A BOULDER RANCH NOVEL

WANT ME

BRITTON BRINKLEY

WANT ME

A BOULDER RANCH NOVEL

BRITTON BRINKLEY

LANDINGHAM STANLEY PRESS

BOULDER RANCH NOVELS

Ride Me by Britton Brinkley

Buck Me by Ashley Willow

Want Me by Britton Brinkley

Love Me by Ashley Willow

Save Me by Britton Brinkley

Hunt Me by Ashley Willow

Shoot your shot; you just might get everything you want.

Author's Note

Delulu until it's trululu. That's the Roberts Row way.

If you're new to the Boulder Ranch franchise, welcome. If you read Ride Me, this book is not that. Gray and River had a pretty clean romance, but Betty and Nash don't. They both learned to live for other people a long time ago, and through their pasts and current situation they'll learn to live for themselves.

Bottom line, Ashley and I are still in our cowboy era and loving it.

Keep in mind Cole County is some random place the Row made up. We don't actually even know what state it's in, so if it sounds familiar, it's a coincidence. Lastly, Boulder Ranch has nothing to do with Colorado.

Get your boots on! The ride is about to start!

Content/Trigger Warnings:
- miscarriage (mentioned)

- abortion (mentioned)

- light breeding kink

- pregnancy

- animal breeding (mentioned)

<u>For the most up-to-date content/trigger warnings:</u>

WANT ME PLAYLIST

Check out my personal Want Me soundtrack.

PROLOGUE

NASH

8 months ago...

My teeth grind as I shoulder my way through the crowd of men lingering just inside the Thirsty Pony doors. Irritation courses through me, knowing I'd let duty to everyone but myself bring me to this damn party tonight.

My father insisted I do the proper thing and blend in with the locals. They're supposed to be my people, too. *"You grew up here just like the rest of us, so you damn well need to act like it,"* he'd quipped, shoving me out the front door. *"Nash, they know you, but they need to get to know you."*

His words struck a chord within my chest. A message like that would have sounded cryptic to anyone else, but I knew exactly what he meant. They might all know I'm his son and I'll be running the business now, but he's always been that degree of separation. I didn't have to be one of them because my father was.

I'd felt cornered when Grayson Garrison boasted about his soon-to-be wife's celebratory party at the Thirsty Pony tonight. The guy's newfound happiness was almost infectious, but not enough for me to want to be here.

Crowds and bars are not my scene. A stranger's skin touching mine, and their warm breath on my neck, makes me twitch. I prefer to be at home or on the ranch. Who the hell would choose to be surrounded by a group of drunk people over the silence or fresh air?

Rechecking my phone, I know it's too early to leave. It doesn't matter if I walked through the door ten minutes ago or two hours; proper etiquette would keep me stuck here until I've seen the right people.

In small-town counties like this, it's not enough to make an appearance. There are hands to shake and faces you absolutely must see before you can call it a night. My childhood buddy, Beckett Hughes, is one of them. No doubt he got stuck working late at the law firm, leaving me to disappear into some dark corner attempting to avoid all of my father's "friends."

Sliding onto a barstool, I flag over the bartender. The guy waves his hand at me, signaling me to wait a minute while he talks to some female behind the counter who's clearly arguing with him. Whatever it is, they need to hurry it along. A few cold ones are the only way I'm surviving tonight.

My fingers tap the bar top with an anxious beat watching them continue their disagreement. Only when she spins around, snatching her bag from beneath the bar with that defeated look on her face, do I notice that it's Betty.

"Betty!" I call out to her, thankful for a familiar face. Beatrice "Betty" Hughes is Beckett's younger sister. I'd been around her plenty as she was growing up, but she was only nine or ten when I first met her. Over the years, I've seen her here and there, especially when I was invited over for Sunday dinners, but as my eyes rake down her body now, it seems like ages.

As Beckett's baby sister, she was almost like mine, too. As time passed, we remained distant friends, always cordial, often cracking jokes. Watching her grin stretch wide when she locks eyes with me causes me to sit a little straighter tonight, though I don't know why.

"Oh wow, Nash!" she gasps, coming around the bar and wrapping me in a hug. "I didn't know you were in town."

My palms lightly press against her mid-back before we release one another. "Yeah, the business is mine now, so I'll be around a lot more."

She grins again, nodding, and I swear a flush creeps over her cheeks. "That's great. Really great." Those doe-brown eyes stare into mine, her lips parting as if she has more to say, but she remains silent for a beat. "I'm, uh... I'm going to find River." Pointing a thumb over her shoulder, she keeps her back to the crowd, slowly backing away. Only when she's made it just out of reach does she spin on her heel, casting one last glance over her bare shoulder. Then she's gone.

Dammit. I'd been hopeful she'd stick around when I saw her, but the woman ran off like talking to me was the last thing she'd ever want to do. Growing up, she couldn't wait to corner me and tell me all the new facts about galaxies and the planets she'd learned. I admit I loved those moments. Witnessing such a young person so passionate about something gave me hope that someday I'd find it too.

But she's gone. There's no one here to entertain me and serve as a block except me. It's only a matter of time before someone slides onto the stool beside me, clapping me on the shoulder, thinking they'll ease into their endless questions about roughstock by pretending to want to know about me. The tactic is dated, and it's the part of the distribution business I've always hated most. I wanted to be out there getting my hands dirty, doing the real work and making the choices, not shaking hands.

Finally, securing my first beer, I stew with my thoughts, refusing to linger on the time passing.

An hour whistles by before Beckett shows, only gracing me with his presence for twenty minutes. Our conversation fizzles and dies the moment a dark-haired beauty slides up next to him at the bar. The two weave their way out to the dance floor, line dancing until sweat coats their skin.

Allowing my gaze to roam over the room, I spot Betty. Her waves are loose, and that broad grin she's always worn is as bright as ever. She cackles loudly with a group of women, including River Thompson, Gray's fiancé. No doubt they're wasted as they attempt to dance their way through each song.

River and Betty are a mess with their locked arms as they stumble over each other's feet. Yet, the corner of my mouth tugs high, watching it. Betty was always the life of the party. The fun one everyone wanted to be around. It shouldn't surprise me that's still true.

I only shake my head, chuckling as I take a swig of my beer. "Hey, Nash!" Beckett's palm clamps down on my shoulder. "I'm going to get out of here." That woman lingers behind him, causing relief to uncoil my shoulders. He doesn't do this often, but it always seems to be on the nights he's roped me into going. Mind you, he isn't responsible for tonight, but he'd been too excited to have me here while he still licks his wounds over River. We all have someone we may never get over, and she's his.

Thinking his departure is my ticket to leave, too, he ruins it the moment he opens his mouth again. "Betty is drunk-drunk. Can you keep an eye on her? Make sure she gets home okay?"

Fuck. Fuck. Fuck.

I only nod before we wrap one another in a one-armed hug, and he shuttles the woman out of the bar. The Hughes family means everything to me, and I'd do anything for them, but tonight I just want to go home and sleep.

Finishing off my beer, I make my way over to Betty, just as the music switches to a slow song.

"Nash!" Betty and River shout my name in unison.

I give an awkward wave as I attempt to lean down and whisper in Betty's ear. My eyes press shut, and my features scrunch as River shouts too close to mine. "Nash, you have to dance with Betty!" Shoving the two of us together, Betty's eyes turn to saucers, her fingers gripping my forearms so tight the woman might draw blood.

"Shall we?" I almost grumble. Soft fingers settle in my extended palm as she nods with a shy grin.

Our feet tangle as I move us toward the dance floor, Betty nearly toppling over as she fights for balance. Grabbing hold of her waist, her eyes meet mine. An emotion I'm convinced I imagined passes behind them, and then it's gone the moment she looks away.

We sway to the beat. No way I'm trying a real slow-dance or two step when she's this drunk. The emergency room is not where I'm ending tonight. Hand still on her waist, I keep her close, allowing her to lean against me for support.

"You're pretty," she grins up at me, her arms looped around my neck.

I've never looked at Betty as anything more than a younger sister. She always seemed that way, given our eight-year age difference, but despite her drunken, flushed cheeks, she has grown into a beautiful woman. There's no denying it. Her body is insane, and her brown eyes seem to sparkle like the stars she was obsessed with.

"Thanks," I snort.

She nods, continuing to stare up at me. One song merges into another, but I hold her closer with each one. For an unwanted babysitting gig, this definitely isn't the worst.

"You know, Nash, you're the man of my dreams. I've thought about you every day since I was ten years old. Do you know what it's like being in love with someone for so long and they don't know?" she snickers to herself, before her fingers sink into my hair. "Well, now you do, I think. Yeah, I'm in love with you, Nash, and there's no one I want more than you."

Fuck. I didn't sign up for this.

CHAPTER 1

BETTY

C offee.

I need coffee.

A massive quadruple-shot coffee.

Give it to me, black as night. Maybe then I won't feel like the walking dead.

Two months ago, when I agreed to take on the manager position here at Boulder Ranch for the new B&B and cabins, I thought nothing of it. River asked for help. I said yes. It's what I do. How hard could it be to run a few bedrooms in the Miller house and some cabins?

Though the job seemed simple enough—checking the cowboys in and out and ensuring everything functioned in the houses—it was also a potential ticket to freedom. I've been working at the Thirsty Pony since I was eighteen. But lately I've been itching for more.

At the time, it was some easy cash while I was in college studying astronomy, and then I never left. It's easy to find comfort in what you know in a place like Cole County. Plus, staying in this small town was always my fate. The Hugheses don't leave Cole County, but I could leave the bar. I could find something I love versus the only future I thought I could have. The weight of mindlessly serving drinks and smiling when I didn't want to was slowly bringing me to my knees.

Over time, the only force that kept me walking through those doors night after night was loyalty. The same loyalty I've always believed I owed to the Hughes name. It didn't matter that I yearned for something different, something more. Cole County and that bar kept me chained right where I was.

Who am I kidding? They still do.

"Oh, wait! No." I charge forward as the movers carry couches toward the newly converted Miller house. "Those go in the cabins out back."

The guy grunts at me, cocking his head to the side, signaling his men to follow.

As I turn to watch them haul pieces of the matching taupe L-shaped couches that will be in each of the six cottages, I'm questioning what I agreed to. Did I give myself yet another entity to pour my loyalty into?

Somehow, I expected to show up on day one, make sure things were in order, check reservations, and then go home at night.

But when the Garrisons handed me the keys, they meant the entire operation. From the day construction started until the day I quit, Miller Inn is mine.

Patting my pocket, the sharp edges of those keys poke my thigh. We'd digitized everything with keypads, linking them to a central tablet, but I've kept the original keys in my pocket every day like a personal good luck charm.

With only a week before the Boulder Ranch rodeo season begins, the pressure of my opening night looms over me. There were several speed bumps along the way. The horrid winter weather, combined with conditions too wet for construction and the wrong materials shipped, inevitably delayed our progress. That's why we're seven days from opening, and I'm just getting furniture for the dang cottages.

Sadie Dillard, River's childhood friend, was here yesterday setting up all the computer systems and tracking programs I'd need to manage the place. Thank goodness for her. I can navigate those sorts of things just fine, but the configuration is way over my head.

I'd stared at her overly round belly the entire time. The thing protruding so far, I'd once again asked her if she was having multiple babies. Instinctively, I'd rubbed the expanse of my soft stomach, the memories threatening to take over my mind. But I didn't let them. I couldn't. There was too much to do, and Betty needed to be chipper and on her game.

"Just one," she'd groaned, attempting to stand from my desk chair.

The crunch of gravel has me spinning back toward the drive in front of the house. Thoughts of babies fade with the familiarity of the truck idling mere feet from me.

That uncontrollable patter of my heart has me wanting to run, but also stay put at the same time.

It's him. *Nash.*

The past eight months have been a duck-and-run-for-cover mission. The few times we've crossed paths since River's party last summer nearly had me vomiting on my shoes in embarrassment as my nerves fired with untameable panic.

I may not remember that portion of the night when Nash danced with me, but he does. River was the one to tell me about my brutal confession of my love for the man who stole my heart when I was ten years old. For that night, I felt like the old Betty. Like there were so many possibilities ahead of me, so I pounded shot after shot with the girls and pretended.

When River told me I'd made a fool of myself, I was mortified.

I've never told a soul how long I've been pining after Nash. He was the initials inside the hearts I drew in my notebooks and the reason I put on pretty dresses for Sunday dinner. No boyfriend has ever compared to the fantasies of Nash in my head. He has consumed my every thought and owned my heart since the day we met, and no one knew but me.

"Hey, Betty." His gruff voice pulls me out of my thoughts.

Slipping my hands in my back pockets, my gaze rakes over his wild, dark umber hair and the perfectly sculpted beard, cropped close to the bottom half of his face. I blink several times, unsure how long I've been standing here like a deer in the headlights. "Um, hi, Nash." Yanking my hands free, they aggressively run down my bare thighs, the humidity higher than usual for April. My clothing feels wet against my skin, or maybe I'm just sweating profusely, staring up at the most handsome face I've ever known.

It was warm enough that I had to pull the cut-off shorts out early. My fitted tee does little to hide the pump of my chest as he takes another step closer.

You need to breathe, Betty.

"The place looks nice." He cocks his head toward the house, his hands slipping into the front pockets of his perfectly fitted jeans.

There's no stopping my gaze from raking down his powerful thighs wrapped in denim. I'm practically salivating imagining what it must have been like to have his body against mine on the dance floor. Pressing my eyes shut, I inhale deeply, forcing my focus to the trees in the distance over his broad shoulder.

Forcing a wide grin, our eyes lock. "Uh, yeah. Hoping it'll be ready for opening weekend."

"It's not now?" Nash's brow knits as he seems to search the grounds for answers.

"Uh, no. The furniture just started arriving today. It'll all be here by Thursday." The mundane nature of the conversation allows me to breathe. My muscles uncoiling, no longer fearing he might bring up that night.

"Damn," he waves his cream cowboy hat, running his fingers through his thick, dark hair.

Taking a discreet step back, I slip my hands into my back pockets once more. My fingers are too eager to run through his hair, too. "What's going on?"

"Garrison said I could stay here for a few days. Looking at a couple of their calves for training." There's nothing but the cold clip of business in his tone. His jaw working as if trying to find another solution.

"Here?" I nearly choke. "Like in the house?"

"Yes. In the house." The words are clipped, a hint of annoyance creeping in. He was never one to pretend to stay calm when his plans went awry.

"Uh, well, there are no beds yet. Um, just in my room. There are couches, though." My voice quivers. If Tate or Gray said he could stay, then I'll need to find a way to make it work. I don't want them firing me before the place even opens.

"You live here?" he questions.

"Uh, no. No, I just—" a heavy sigh releases from me, Nash looking away as if annoyed we're still standing out here in the sweltering wet heat. "I stay when I need to."

"No worries. Couch is fine," he grunts, turning back to his truck and pulling an overnight bag free.

"Right, uh. You can let yourself in."

"Right. Okay. Bye, Betty."

He moves around me, my eyes pressing shut again, trying to force breaths into my lungs.

He'd been so normal. So unaffected—I think. But dammit, I couldn't even get out complete sentences half the time.

Embarrassment causes my chest to pump faster than it should. My heart can't handle being under the same roof as Nash tonight. Likely not ever.

Swiping flyaways off my face, I suck in several soul-cleansing breaths. Focus. That's what I need.

He'd been so normal. He'd been the same Nash I've always known. How could he know how I feel about him and be completely unaffected?

How could he say nothing about it?

Smiling wide as another delivery truck pulls up, I do my best to push Nash Donovan out of my mind. I have a job to do, and it has nothing to do with obsessing over a man who couldn't care less about me.

My temples ache, and stale sweat sticks to my skin. Three hours of directing delivery people in this humidity nearly had me fainting in the yard. It seemed to be endless as they hauled in tables, chairs, couches, and decor: everything but the damn beds.

It was an uphill battle transferring between departments, with each taking a turn to provide no help, before a manager confirmed Thursday as the soonest possible date. There were delays with the suppliers, *blah, blah, blah*. The reason didn't matter. Our first guests are checking in next Friday, and I need to have a place for them to sleep—end of story.

River has become my best friend, and the last thing I want to do is let her or her newly minted husband down. They vouched for me to Tate. In truth, I'm not sure he cared who his brother hired as long as it wasn't one more thing for him to think about.

Grumbling sounds fill the air as I rub my stomach, shuffling toward the kitchen. Breakfast and coffee never happened this morning. Forget food, I need that boost of energy if I'm going to get any work done tonight.

Turning the corner into the massive kitchen area, the sweet aroma of food and dark roast coffee wafts up my nostrils. My stomach growls again, the sound so loud that whoever is in the kitchen must have heard it. The Garrisons insisted that as long as the ranch folks cleaned up after themselves, they had free rein to use the kitchen at their leisure.

For the second time today, I'm anchored in place. Nash moves through the kitchen as if he lives here, cooking steaks on the stove before pouring a large mug of coffee. The scent of the herbs assaults me, and I want nothing more than to shovel his food into my mouth.

"Thought you might need this," he says without even looking up.

"No." The word blurts out of my mouth despite it watering in anticipation of that tender meat and the bitter bite of caffeine. The gesture, though kind, is making my head spin, and I don't know what to do about it. Not when he knows and hasn't said a word. "I'm fine," I lie.

The words had come out squeaky and uneven, but I don't leave myself time to obsess over them. Spinning on my heel, I'm ready to bolt to the room that was claimed as mine when Nash's voice makes me stop in my tracks.

"It's fine, yah know. I'm not gonna treat you any differently because of what you told me." Tenderness coats his words, that big-brother tone wrapping each one in a protective blanket.

Again, my eyes press shut, tears burning and threatening to break free.

If only he understood that's the problem.

In a perfect world or a rom-com, I would have confessed my love, and he'd have swept me off my feet. We'd live happily ever after, and for once, I'd have everything I wanted.

Reality isn't a neatly wrapped package with a pristine bow, though.

I say nothing as I blink away my tears and wander toward my bedroom.

One day, I'll get Nash Donovan out of my system. I have to. Because no matter what I do, he's never going to want me.

CHAPTER 2

NASH

Each muscle quivers as I push against the soft ground beneath my palms. My lungs burn through every grunted exhale, but I keep pushing. Every power push-up rep threatens to leave me face-first in the mud. Curling up on that damn couch last night already put me at a disadvantage, leaving my body an achy mess this morning. This frame isn't made for shit like that anymore.

By the time I'd found the energy to sit up just as dawn crept over the horizon, I felt like someone had taken a sledgehammer to my limbs. Still, I knew I needed this. I needed the burn and the chance to clear my head.

Though maybe I wouldn't have needed to punish my body at all if Betty hadn't had on that tight top and those tiny cut-off shorts. *Fuck*, it took everything in me not to get hard taking in the curves of her lean muscle. Every droplet of sweat down her chin that fell between her breasts could have been water on my tongue.

Objectively, Betty has always been a beautiful girl. The entire Hughes family could be models if they ever left this damn county. But when I saw her yesterday and didn't immediately cut off those wayward thoughts, my mind went haywire. They consumed me, fantasizing about all the filthy things I wanted to do to her.

It didn't matter that I called her a kid in my head, though she's in her thirties now. It doesn't matter that I told myself she's my buddy's baby sister and I shouldn't look at her that way. I wanted to act on her attraction. I have since September, when I ran into her at the ranch and she'd been clad in jeans that looked painted on, showcasing the round curve of her perfect ass.

It was the first time I saw her after her confession at River's party. I didn't know what to say to her that night. Not that it would have mattered. She'd been drunk out of her mind.

I blame myself for her baring her soul that night. Treating her like we were old friends while I held her close on the dance floor had been wrong.

Hours have passed while I lay awake staring at the ceiling, trying to understand how I didn't know. How could I have missed the way she looked at me for years?

But now it's different.

There's heartbreak nearly drowning out her longing stare. A stare I never realized I've known since the first night I stayed over at her house back in high school.

The Hughes house quickly became our team gathering spot when Beckett made the football team. It was summer training, and Mrs. Hughes offered to host the team's sleepover. They grilled us enough food to feed an army and showered us with snacks. It was one of the most fun nights I had in high school.

From as young as I can remember, I've always woken up in the middle of the night in search of water. That's when I found her outside, just staring up at the sky. It wasn't something I lingered over then. The cute little ten-year-old was tracing the stars with her finger. An act so innocent it made me smile.

"You okay?" I'd asked.

She only nodded, but didn't stop her fingers moving through the air, that goofy grin lighting up her face. *"I always come out here when the moon is gone. It's when I can see the stars best."*

I'd left her there, crept back into the house, grabbed a glass of water, and then shimmied back into my sleeping bag. The next morning was the first time she looked at me like there were stars in her eyes. A kiddy crush. We've all had one.

I just never knew it stuck around for twenty-three years.

"Might want to save some of that energy for wrangling calves," Gray chuckles, his shadow looming over me with his hands on his hips.

"Mornin' to you too," I grunt, pumping out another set of twenty before slowly climbing to my feet.

I'm completely wiped. Every bit of energy I had is gone. A necessary evil, so I could stop thinking about that woman still asleep in her room inside the Miller house.

"You wanna talk about it?" Gray leans against my truck, crossing his arms over his chest.

Wiping sweat from my forehead with the back of my hand, I stalk toward the house. "Nope. Let me change, and we can get started."

The house is quiet when I enter. No matter how I try to stifle my movements, rifling through my overnight bag for clothing and my toiletries case is like a booming chorus of sound.

The full bath on the first floor is right beside Betty's room. I can only hope she sleeps like the dead; the last thing I want to do is wake her. If she looks at me with those pleading brown eyes again, I won't be able to resist her.

Fuck, I'm barely hanging on now. Fantasies of her hold me at their mercy as they once again float through my head. So much for punishing it out of my system.

Slipping through the bathroom door, I close it with the softest click. My eyes stay glued to the natural plank of wood, each step carrying me further away. I refuse to turn my back toward it as if she's going to burst through the door at any moment.

And do what, Nash? You broke her heart. She isn't going to fuck you.

Minutes pass of staring straight ahead before I release a ragged sigh. Dropping my shit on the side table, I scrub my hands over my face. The muscles in my neck seem to revolt as I slowly lift my gaze before stumbling back several feet.

"What the hell are you doing in here?" Betty snaps, moving out of the alcove where the Jack and Jill sinks sit.

My eyes dart around the room as if the walls hold the answer to her question. I'm wondering if they remodeled the bathroom now. The toilet also has its own alcove, and the shower is on the opposite wall, with a large tub serving as the background when you're facing the mirror.

"I—I, uh, was showering."

"Can you wait until I'm done or go upstairs?" For the first time, she stares at me like she actually wants me gone. And, fuck do I hate that.

"Yeah. 'Course." But I don't move, staring at her bare legs on display beneath a Cole County High football t-shirt. A shirt she must have had from when Beckett was on the team.

"Nash!" she snaps. "Get out." Her eyes meet mine. "Please."

"I'm sorry," I say, scooping up my things and rushing out of the bathroom. Jogging up the stairs two at a time, I can't understand why my interaction with Betty rattles me. I promised nothing would be awkward, and that's exactly what it's been. I fucking hate it.

In less than ten minutes, I'm showered and changed only to find Gray chatting with one of the ranch hands, still leaning against my truck.

Without a word, the three of us make our way out to the fields. The more distance we put between us and the Miller house, the more my focus locks into place. Gray and Beau are efficient as they walk me through the pedigrees for the calves that the Garrisons asked me to evaluate. Several have what we'd consider strong bloodlines, the perfect mix for training as rodeo competitors.

By the time we're finished, all I want to do is curl up on that uncomfortable couch again and sleep for a year. I'd skipped coffee this morning, eager to get out of the house. It was as if being in her vicinity wound me up to the point I couldn't breathe. A response I am stuck wracking my brain trying to understand. I don't see her that way. There's no chance of a relationship or anything between us, so why do I care so damn much?

There should be a way to explain it to her, but I can't find the words. No matter how attractive she might be to me, we won't work. Betty is kind, sweet, and young. She doesn't want a man like me. She just doesn't know that yet.

Gray claps me on the shoulder as we march back to the house. "Come have a beer with us," he grumbles. His buddy Beau nods along like a damn bobblehead, the gesture causing me to groan loudly.

Every fiber is still sore as hell, and I'm already exhausted from the flight out here yesterday.

"I think I'm gonna get some sleep. We wrapped up everything we needed to do today, so I am gonna try to head back to Montana tomorrow." The thought of attempting to find a different flight makes me groan again. This back and forth is going to wear on me real quick. It didn't seem like it would be any worse than the travel I often do now, but coming home always takes a little something extra out of me. It's a constant reminder of what I promised I'd never leave behind.

"All the more reason to have a beer with us now. Next weekend will be too busy," Beau interjects. I've only met the guy a few times. He's the last person who could get me to venture to a bar.

We clear the hill to the east of the house, Betty coming into view. Instead of those shorts, she has on a sundress. The type that appears innocent, but you can't wait to whip up once your woman is bent over the bed of your truck while you drive into her from behind.

That used to be my life. A long time ago. A lifetime ago.

A soft breeze whips through her loose waves and the bottom of the dress. My cock is twitching in my jeans, wondering what's underneath. *Briefs. Boyshorts. Thong. Nothing.*

An audible groan leaves me. "You good?" Gray snorts.

"Uh, yeah. Just sore as hell. Let's get that beer. I'll drive."

The three of us cut left, jumping in my truck without so much as another word.

But I feel her eyes on me. And when I look in the rearview mirror, all I see is her.

CHAPTER 3

BETTY

From the very first moment I walked into the Thirsty Pony holding my hand-written paper application, I wasn't nervous. When I faced my first astronomy exam in college, I felt only excitement. Yet now, as I sit on the Miller house sofa, my hands knot in my lap, and anxious butterflies soar through my stomach.

My palms sweat, knowing that in a matter of moments, our first guest will arrive. Though I've never been close to the Garrison brothers, letting them down in any way is not something I am willing to do. Worrying my bottom lip, I shoot to my feet for the tenth time, pacing the short distance between where the cream and brown rug meets the original natural oak hardwood floors.

It's been months of watching this place come together. Months of organizing every detail and ensuring we were not only serving those who come to compete or vendor for the rodeo, but also the business. That's how Tate asked me to look at this. Boulder Ranch may be a place for family, but it has to be more than that if it's going to survive and then thrive.

I've only just slumped back onto the opposite couch when the sharp crack of a knock at the door launches me back to my feet. My body involuntarily jumps as if I hadn't expected a guest to arrive.

Smoothing the simple business casual dress down my thighs, my heart rate instantly races, hoping I didn't leave palm prints on the soft green fabric. The heels River insisted I wear click across the floor as I make my way to the door, swinging it wide.

My classic Betty grin stretches across my face as the stranger comes into view. "Welcome to Boulder Ranch." Flashing all of my teeth, the young cowboy on the other side immediately smiles back. His crooked grin is the type that could make a woman blush, but not this one. Not when a piece of me was hoping it would be Nash coming to sweep me off my feet, knowing that was never going to happen.

"Howdy, ma'am," he drawls, removing his hat while briefly dipping his chin in greeting. His grin matches mine, wide and forthcoming. Only his appears genuine, while mine is the practiced expression I mastered before I even entered high school.

I'd thought it would be hard to turn on the charm after being away from the bar these past few months, but it came naturally. Perhaps I shouldn't have doubted myself when this is who I've always been to everyone around me.

But the optimist in me hopes it's the excitement of working with people drawing out my natural joy. When it was time to find my first job, I knew it was a must. I may not have always felt like the fun girl everyone thought I was, but I endured because I've always loved being there for others and helping them through life. Looking back, a people-pleaser like me might see it that way.

"Please come in." Gesturing my arm to the side as I angle my body out of the doorway, he quickly steps over the threshold. A ratty brown duffel bag hangs over his shoulder, likely some sort of good luck charm he refuses to travel without. "Name?" I ask, moving ahead toward my laptop, which I left on the living room coffee table.

"Ward. Ward Ferrell," his deep baritone hits me from behind. His presence at my back has my nerve endings crackling with awareness. *Weird.*

Spinning to face him, he's closer, but not intrusively so. It's a respectful distance with his hat still poised over his stomach. The last man, aside from my brother and father, I was this close to was Nash.

Dammit, I need him out of my head.

"Alright, Mr. Ferrell, I have you out in cabin 1A. There are no keys. The code is seven-five-three-seven for the front door.

If you need anything, I'm usually here at the main house, or you can find my phone number in the reservation email."

Soft hazel eyes meet mine, that crooked grin pulling a fraction higher. "Is that your personal number?" His tone is hopeful, as if he genuinely wants to know. Usually, I would be creeped out by now, but there's something trustworthy about the man standing in front of me.

A flush creeps up my chest and neck, flooding my cheeks with color. It's not that I don't get hit on. I do. All the time. Some I'll date, but most I compare to Nash and decide they're not worth my time. Which, looking back now, was stupid. I barely know the man now, yet my heart has always belonged to him.

With an awkward laugh, I place my laptop back on the table. "They are one and the same; however, let's keep it to business."

"'Course." He nods, his own face growing pink as if embarrassed. "But can I at least know your name?"

"Beatrice. Uh, Betty. Everyone just calls me Betty." A heavy breath releases from me as I clutch the tablet in both palms in front of my thighs.

"See ya around, Beatrice." Then he's back out the door, following the newly graveled paths to the cabins that sit behind the Miller house.

From the side windows, I can watch him until he disappears inside the cabin at the end. I allow myself to get lost in my mind, thinking about the handsome cowboy out back. He'd seemed kind enough. Maybe I should have been bolder and told him to use it anytime. Maybe it would make me forget that Nash has never and will never want anything to do with me.

But I can't.

I've tried—countless times. Even Ryan, a man I was planning to marry, couldn't erase Nash from my heart and mind.

Every boyfriend who dumped me, knowing they weren't the man I was thinking of when they held me at night or we had sex, could tell you so. It was always him. Always fucking Nash with that winning grin burned on my soul.

So I let myself think of Ward. Of possibilities, as a wide grin stretches the corners of my mouth when the front door opens.

"Betty?"

An audible gasp leaves me, my eyes gaping at the man before me. Good grief, did my thoughts summon him or something? "Nash? What are you doing here?" I immediately stand, my mouth pressed into a straight line as I stare into those blue eyes I've been lost in my whole life.

"I'm staying here," he answers dryly. No inflection. No emotion. Not even a proper hello.

My heart fractures a little more, and my hope withers and dies.

It's not like I didn't know he was a guest this weekend. I did. And I purposely sent him an extra email with his cabin information ahead of time to avoid moments like this. "You already have your cabin information."

He steps closer, his woodsy scent wafting up my nose. It's a fight not to inhale deeply. Not to fist his shirt and breathe him in like I've always wanted to. "Yeah, but I was hoping you could make a switch," he mutters.

"Oh, why?"

He's suddenly another step closer, and the multicolored hues of his eyes become clear. *Don't stare, Betty.* "I really wanted the first cabin at the end. Quieter. More privacy." His tone hasn't changed since the moment he walked through the door. I can't recall a time he has ever been so dry with me, but I've also never seen him so worn down.

"Privacy for what? The women you plan on bringing back with you?" My hand clamps over my mouth. There's no chance the universe will answer my wish and erase the last five seconds. My body heats with the flames of embarrassment as Nash's eyes gape wide, not just in shock but with mirth dancing there.

"No," he chuckles. "The young rodeo guys like to party. I like to sleep."

"Of course. I'm so sorry. I, well, yeah. Cabin 1B. The code is seven-five-three-seven," I quickly blurt out, tumbling over my words. Anything to get me out of this situation as fast as possible.

Something flashes in his eyes as I relay the numbers. It's the same stare we've shared in the last few encounters we've had. Our lips part, and our breathing shifts as if we're both going to confess, then one of us breaks eye contact, and the moment is over.

Today it's him.

"Thanks." He tips his head to me before reaching for the front door. "If you need a ride to the Thirsty Pony tonight, you come find me."

"I won't. Beckett will be here."

"Beckett?" Nash spins back to face me. "Damn, I haven't seen him since..." A genuine smile stretches wide, the corners of his eyes crinkling, aging him just before he finishes his statement. The night I ruined everything.

Studying Nash's face now, I've never thought about how time has changed us because it wasn't just his looks I cared about. I've always seen Nash as the eighteen-year-old boy who checked on me in the middle of the night, but he's forty now. Neither of us are those same children anymore.

"Well, you'll see him at the bar tonight. Sorry, but I have work to do. You have my number if you need anything."

His jaw flexes, eyes casting down to where my chest pumps heavily. "Yeah, Betty. I do." Then he's gone, too.

I scrub my hands over my face, not caring if I smudge the soft nude eyeshadow or my mascara. How am I going to survive an entire season with Nash here all the damn time?

If only I hadn't confessed. Not that it would have changed a thing. I'd still be here, pining after a man who doesn't want me.

Rolling my shoulders back, I make a choice.

No more.

I've wasted too many thoughts, breaths, and dreams on Nash Donovan. If he saw me as anything more, he would have said something at the very least.

What are those song lyrics? *If he wanted to, he would.*

He doesn't.

CHAPTER 4

NASH

I can understand why the distribution business ran my father into the ground. Mind you, I still live in Montana full-time. Driving or flying halfway across the country to get here for rodeo weekends takes its toll. But rodeo nights themselves are beyond exhausting.

And tonight wasn't even the real deal. I haven't been to an opening night since my sophomore year in college. Pop was tucked in bed, shivering from the flu, and needed my help, so I was here. He had others who were more active in the business than I was, so I was more of an assistant than the head of the team.

"This will all be yours one day," he'd said. *"Pay attention."*

Yet, at the time, I didn't feel the dread and expectations of having to fill his shoes. There was just enough room to distance myself and pretend it would be a lifetime before I had to live up to him and my grandfather's image.

That's different now. Pop is retired, and it's all me. I'm in charge. I call the shots. It's me working with the various promotions and keeping the stock ready to go. We primarily supply bulls, but also offer a select number of calves and saddle bronc horses when needed.

I've been running around like a madman, checking in with everyone to ensure I don't fuck this up. I can't. It's my family's legacy. There's pressure that comes with that truth, a pressure I never felt when I started my own company. In a way, it seemed as if there was no one to disappoint but me, though that's a lie.

When it came time for college, I didn't hesitate to leave this county behind. It was my one chance to be someone else, somewhere else, before the family legacy sucked me back in. Yet, the need to escape never changed how I felt about family. They are everything. My backbone, my reason why. I would do anything for them. Be anywhere for them. Be anyone...

That's what I'd hoped to build with Katherine—our own family. Life didn't work out that way, though. Many say to marry your best friend. That's the recipe for success. We did that, and still we drifted apart. No one was right or wrong. There was no animosity. Just the towel thrown in after a decade of marriage and even more years of memories.

I haven't dated another woman since. There's been no time or interest, until now...

Exhaustion keeps me yawning as I enter the Thirsty Pony with a few of the guys on my heels. They're all recapping the competitors who took part tonight—the amateurs. Tomorrow is the real deal. The paid competitors. The ones that help put our stock on the map for other promotions when they perform well.

I've barely made it through the door when Beckett appears out of nowhere, pulling me into a one-armed hug. "Nash! Damn, it's good to see you."

The scent of whiskey is strong on his breath. Not a surprise. Most will have already been here for an hour or two after the rodeo ended. It's those of us who work who take longer to arrive, and we are expected to attend, with no exceptions. It's tradition.

Beckett pulls me toward a table in the back corner, Betty and River laughing loudly, while Gray rubs circles into River's back. He throws me a two-finger salute, his eyes never leaving his wife.

I'd heard Beckett was still hung up on River, so I'm surprised to see them all together, but maybe it's that whole family first thing again. Beckett would do anything for his baby sister.

Remember that Nash. She's his baby sister, not a woman you can fuck until she forgets her name.

Shaking the thoughts clear, I take a seat, clasping hands with Gray and waving to River.

"Great night tonight," Gray shouts over the thrumming music and chatter.

"Yeah. That was the best performance I've seen from Mr. Knight. The big promotions had their eyes on him before, but didn't think he had enough agility. Tonight proved them wrong." I can't help but grin knowing one of our bulls pulled the highest score tonight.

We're not the only distributor. There will always be others, but my father made it a mission to be the dependable one these rodeos and promotions could call. That's a legacy I won't let go to waste.

"Betty, you didn't even say hi to Nash." Beckett knocks her arm.

Not once does she look my way, her eyes pleading with River beside her. "Time to dance," River bolts from her seat, grabbing Betty's hand and pulling her along. The three of us watch our women. Gray and Beckett focused on River, while my gaze lingers on Betty.

We'd run into each other during the rodeo, too, but she'd kept the conversation brief. The usual small-talk questions about my preparedness for the night and how I slept spewed past her lips as she fought to stare at anything but my face.

It hurt. Betty and I have always had a fun relationship. She never seemed to have any issues chatting my ear off or grabbing me by the shoulders and shaking me playfully. But now, she won't even look at me.

Still, I can't take my eyes off her as she and River stomp in their cowboy boots, laugh, and spin. It seems like every time I lay eyes on her, she's more beautiful than the last. The many conversations we've had over the years resurface in my mind, playing like old movies with flickering images. I miss that version of us.

We watch in silence until a few men join them—one with a hand on Betty's hip and the other reaching for River. Gray's out of his seat in seconds, leveling the guys with his stare. River's laughter is silent but somehow resonates in my chest as she wraps her arms around Gray's neck and kisses him.

Rubbing the heel of my palm over my sternum, I wonder if I'm having my first heart attack at the ripe old age of forty.

The moment reminds me so much of when Katherine and I first met. We were two people having the time of our lives. The laughter never stopped, and the adventures seemed endless.

That trip down memory lane is quickly forgotten as the music changes and the guy who'd touched Betty spins her into his chest. The slow rhythm allows him to hold her close, her eyes trained on his face as they move together.

"That guy is way too close to her," I grunt, expecting Beckett to be on my side.

He only shrugs, taking another swallow of his drink. "She'll always be my baby sister, but honestly, I'm glad she quit working here—mostly. She needs to get out more. Have more fun. Meet someone who is going to take the time to treat her right."

"Has she not been?"

He shakes his head, leaning in a bit closer. "No. She claims the men who take her out are fine, but that's my baby sister. She'll find a way to give it a positive spin because that's what she's always done for everyone around her. To me, they should worship the ground she walks on. Shower her in the love she deserves. They stick around for a few months, maybe a year, and then they bolt."

Somehow, I don't believe the last part, but Beckett's words are the nail in my coffin. If any part of me was thinking I could ever give Betty what she needs now, I know I can't. She needs a heartfelt man. A tender one. One who will make love to her and show up with flowers.

Katherine always told me I wasn't the type for hearts and roses. That I showed love in my own way, but not the fairytale kind that women dreamed about. She was okay with it because she loved me as I was, but looking at the way Betty stares up into the eyes of that stranger, I know I'll never be that for her.

"I need to go," I slam a twenty on the table, though I hadn't even ordered a drink yet.

"What? Why?" Beckett sits upright, his drink sloshing over the rim of his glass.

"I'm exhausted, and tomorrow is another long day." It's the truth, but really it's an excuse. Because if I sit here for one more minute watching another man with his hands on her, I don't know what I'll do. I haven't had such trouble controlling these types of impulses since my college years. Now is not the time to become a possessive man over a woman who can never be mine.

"Okay, well, at least come to the house for Sunday night dinner. I'm sure my parents would love to see you," Beckett adds, relaxing back into his chair.

My chin drops to my chest as I inhale deeply. "Yeah. Fine."

In my heart, I know I'm going to regret this.

CHAPTER 5

NASH

The soft patter of rain hits my shoulders and the exposed skin of my arms as I bolt from the bar.

Why the hell did I say yes to a family dinner at the Hughes house?

I've been there countless times, especially during senior year, and even in the first few years of college, when Beckett and I remained close. He'd been my little protégé back then. A kid himself, he looked up to me, and I was proud to be that role model.

Then, life just changed. Katherine and I moved in together. I was finishing college and then building my consulting business. I still saw the Hughes family around town while I was visiting. They still asked after me to my family, but damn, I don't know the last time I saw them. For years, they were such a fixture in my life, and only now am I realizing that they're not.

How am I going to look into Georgia Hughes's eyes and smile, knowing I've thought about fucking their daughter so hard she won't be able to walk after?

I'll come up with an excuse. I'm needed in Montana, or I'm not feeling well. Too tired. Not hungry.

Mumbling to myself as I climb into my truck, a damp hand on my forearm stops me. I'm half-seated as I look over at those beautiful doe-brown eyes. "Uh, Beckett said you were going to bed." Betty's wide eyes look up at me through her lashes, her fingers flexing slightly against my bare skin, searing my flesh.

"Yeah, tomorrow is a big day. I'm tired." Averting my gaze, I focus on climbing all the way into the truck and starting the engine, ignoring the raindrops hitting the interior door. Ignoring the way she still grips my arm, every muscle flexing as if trying to expose more of me to her touch.

As if burned, she quickly yanks her hand away. "Right. Well, uh, some of the guys were planning to bring the party back to the cabins. You can take my room in the main house."

"Don't you stay there?" I ask, shifting my body in her direction.

The rain starts to fall faster, large droplets hitting her cheeks. Her damp lashes flutter as I reach out to touch her jaw, my thumb stroking the moisture across her skin.

Her breath hitches, but she doesn't pull away.

She doesn't avert her gaze, her chest pumping quickly the way it often does around me. My thumb swipes over the apple of her cheek before she pulls away, taking a step back.

"Only when I need to," she whispers.

"And you don't opening weekend?" I question sliding out of the truck, closing the distance she just put between us. It makes no sense how much I need to be close to her. It's as if I need to be circling her orbit to get a view of her.

"You can take my room," she says again, taking another step back.

I can't help but reach for her, my hand finding her waist, while the other cups her face again. I have no idea what the hell I'm doing. It's wrong to take advantage of my jumbled feelings for her, but I can't help but be attracted to her. It's not like I suddenly became a saint and stopped sleeping with women after my divorce. I just don't date them. I don't have the time or the desire to put myself out there seriously. Not when I am one man in public and another behind closed doors.

Her soft lips part, those eyes never leaving my face.

"Betty."

"Please don't, Nash. I am trying to keep my distance and not make this weird." Her whimper nearly shatters my heart. Of all the people I've crossed paths with in my entire life, Betty has been the kindest. She's the last person I'd ever want to hurt.

"You don't have to avoid me."

Her gaze casts down to her feet, her hands knotting in front of her stomach before she looks up at me again. "Yes, I do. If you're staying at the house, I can't. I always knew you would never see me like that, but then that night, at the party, I remembered how much fun we were having, and my fantasies got away from me. I guess that's why I told you. A part of me thought maybe now I could have you the way I always wanted. But I can't, can I?"

"Betty," I sigh. "I'm not the type of man you need."

"That's what I thought." Her sad smile wobbles, and I would do anything to go back in time to the days when I would be at her house and she would giggle over documentaries. I wish I could go back and have been invisible to her then. I hate that she's carried this flame for me for so long, and I can't give her a damn thing back except a meaningless fuck. "You have the code to the main house. The sheets are clean. Have a good night."

There's nothing to do but watch her walk away. I tell myself it's for the best. Hopefully, she'll never look back. I can't stand breaking that woman's heart any more than I have.

The scent of fresh linen and eucalyptus envelops me as I roll over in bed. Not the bed I was supposed to be sleeping in, but Betty's.

Staring up at the ceiling, I can't help but replay every moment with her since the night she told me she'd been in love with me. Since then, very few of our interactions have been one-on-one. I regret not having tried harder to talk to her. Instead, I let her avoid me as much as she wanted, while I lingered in the shadows, learning everything I could about her.

It surprised me that she's very much the same Betty I always knew. Organized, funny, charming, and witty. The way she latches on to facts and can spew them back to you as if it's nothing always impresses me.

Had she not been so much younger and Beckett's little sister, would I have ever considered her?

Before Betty confessed to me, I couldn't recall a single moment I so much as looked at her as anything other than that ten-year-old girl staring up at the stars. I met her as a kid, and that's where I kept her. She remained that young, curious mind I could sit back and listen to ramble about everything and nothing for hours.

My phone suddenly buzzes on the nightstand, a groan leaving me as I snatch it off the surface.

"Hello."

"Sleeping in, I see?" Hunt chuckles from the other line—my right hand in business.

We met in college, freshman year. He wasn't my roommate, but lived down the hall. It didn't take long for us to forge a bond. Neither of us cared for our assigned roommates and found refuge in each other.

When I first told him I was going into the distribution business with my father, but also consulting on the side, he was the first to cheer me on. His experience in corporate America and prestigious business degree made him my best resource. He'd supported me from afar and then at my side when he quit his soul-sucking job. We've been a pair ever since.

"It was a long night," I groan, digging the heel of my palm into each eye, clearing the sleep.

"Is she still there?" His voice drops as he whispers, but I can hear the laughter in his tone. After my divorce, Hunt has called me plenty of mornings and found me whispering as I stumble around trying to redress after yet another fling or one-night stand.

"It was opening night. You know that," I grunt, throwing my legs over the side of the bed. "Why are you calling me so early?"

A soft hum sounds through the phone as if he's contemplating the mysteries of the universe. "The Langley deal might fall through. Turns out the purchaser can't come up with the funds."

"Shit!"

The soft tap of his finger on a tablet screen fills the brief silence. "Yeah, not ideal. But another buyer will pay almost double if it does." That's Hunt. There's always a Plan B, C, and D. It's not enough to trust someone at their word. He'll be prepared for every scenario and then prepare additional favorable outcomes for the plans we didn't need to use.

"Then why are you calling me?" I groan, ready to fall back into Betty's soft pillows and pretend they're her soft body.

"There's no deal unless they can meet with you in person next week," he sighs.

I want to scream. Heading home to Montana wasn't part of the plan. I'd planned on staying in Cole County for a week or so. It was a perfect excuse to catch up with the family and ensure we're prepared for our event next weekend. Then, maybe, I could spend time with...

No, Nash. No, you're not going near her like that.

"I'll be there."

"Figured as much," Hunt chuckles. "Safe travels, man."

The line goes dead, and I just sit there.

It was my choice to stay in Montana after Katherine and I ended our marriage. When you grow up in a place like Cole County, you either can't wait to get out or you never want to leave. I always felt like something was wrong with me for wanting both of them.

Guilt nearly swallowed me for wanting to see the world, while never wanting to leave my family's farm. I wanted to hike to waterfalls, but not miss my nieces and nephews running around the same land I did as a child—not that we ever get to witness that.

After I graduated, Katherine and I decided to stay in Montana. We'd grown comfortable there. It was affordable to purchase a large amount of land and build the massive modern house she desired. We could live off the map in the silence, but still jet set wherever we wanted because we were at the top of our fields. We were an unstoppable couple—the best of friends.

Funny, after she walked out the front door for the last time, I was convinced the call of Cole County would bring me home. In my mind, I just knew Montana couldn't still feel like home, but somehow it did. A part of me still belonged in that massive house all alone.

Montana had become home as much as Cole County always would be.

Only, for the first time, I'm finding more reasons to stay in this small town. Perhaps the call has finally come, and it's in the form of a woman I never even took notice of.

Fuck me.

CHAPTER 6

BETTY

"Momma," I shout, pushing the front screen door open with my ass, my hands full of grocery bags. The handles painfully dig into my arms, but I refuse to take a second trip back out to the truck. It's principle.

My mother comes bolting around the corner, her galaxy apron tied around her narrow waist and a dish towel slung over her shoulder. "Why are you shoutin'?" It was the first Mother's Day gift I bought her with my own money when I was eighteen. She's worn it every Sunday since.

Georgia Hughes has always been most comfortable in the kitchen. Making us meals and inviting anyone who would come to the house so that she could cook for them, too. It was where she felt most useful from the day she married my father.

They'd planned for a horde of children, but only got the two of us. Years of miscarriages took all the others, but she has never whined or complained. In a way, it was fortunate that I was popular and Beckett was a football player. Teens always filled the house. Their raucous laughter and bottomless stomachs were there for my mother to shower with affection and food. She used to say she was gifted with more children than her womb could ever carry. It was a statement I never understood until she was the person who was there when my entire life fell apart years ago.

"I'm shoutin' because these bags are heavy."

She snatches them from my hands, kissing my cheek before sashaying to the kitchen, with her 90s country music blaring through the house. This is how she's always been. Her fiery but selfless energy fills this house.

Her humming carries back to me as I grab the last bag I had to sit on the front porch before following her to the kitchen. I find her already busy putting away each item as if we aren't going to use them to make dinner in two minutes. "You know you're supposed to cook that?" My nose wrinkles as she *tsks* at me.

"I'm making meatloaf and my special red-skin mashed potatoes," she grins, continuing to organize everything I bought for Chicken Fettuccini Alfredo.

That familiar sensation of my heart seizing in my chest hits me. I try to calm it with a few quick breaths. It's a coincidence. It has to be. Why else would she be making Nash's favorite meal?

"Why are you?" My question stalls on my tongue as the front screen door closes. Heavy footfalls trail through the house before stopping at the kitchen doorway. Pressing my eyes shut, I try to convince myself I'm imagining this. It's not happening. My mind just wants Nash to be here because that means he chose me.

"Mama Hughes?" Nash's voice booms through the space. My eyes fly open, plastered to his face. He's actually here. Why is he here?

I swear, I cannot escape the man. How am I supposed to move on if he's always right there? River and I agreed it's best I let this go. That I allow myself to find someone else who will make me happy.

"Right here, honey." My mom pops up from behind the fridge door, flashing Nash a grin so wide I wonder if she's happier to see him than me.

Waving the bouquet in his hand, with the other tucked behind his back, he greets Mom. "Hey, Mama Hughes," he grins wide, the stubble on his face making him appear as tired as the dark bags under his eyes.

He'd been clean-shaven yesterday. A look I had become accustomed to on him. Sometimes he'd have a mustache, but I can't remember a single time I've seen him with a beard over the years.

"What are you doing here?" I gasp, clutching the grocery bag to my chest as if it's some form of protection.

Other than the five feet of hardwood between us, it is.

"Hey, Betty. Uh, Beckett invited me. I hope I'm not intruding." His gaze meets mine, an emotion flashing and fading so quickly I can convince myself it was never there.

"Nonsense," my mother smacks him with a dishrag before tucking it into her apron. She doesn't hesitate to pull him into a hug. The tight ones that make you feel safe and remind you that you're home. Mom has always given the best hugs. Pulling back from him, she runs a hand along his biceps, the muscles bulging beneath his button-up. "You're never an intruder in this house, Nash. You know that." She smiles widely, sauntering back to the fridge, putting away the ingredients I'd bought that will inevitably not be used for a few days. "Those are some pretty flowers," she adds, "but I don't need them. Betty loves multicolored bouquets, though." She glances over her shoulder, winking before continuing her tasks.

Heat rushes to my cheeks, and all I want to do is hide.

"Thanks, Mama Hughes." He runs his long fingers over his chin. "Uh, actually..." he pauses, spinning to face me fully, extending his arm. "Betty, I actually brought these for you."

My heart pounds in my chest. The rhythm is so erratic, I'm debating calling River to make sure I'm not having a heart attack. My body is on fire, not in the way that's caused by pleasure, but embarrassment.

"Thank you," I slowly take the flowers from his extended hand, our fingers brushing. A fresh wave of heat and a zap of lightning zip through my body. "And thank you for coming. I didn't mean to sound rude."

"Don't apologize. Put me to work." That grin spreads again. The one I've known my whole life. It's warm and inviting. When I was younger, it instilled in me a belief in kindness. Now it makes the muscles in my lower belly tighten as my arousal soaks my underwear.

Dammit.

"Nonsense," my mother waves him off again. "Dinner is almost ready. It's your favorite Nash." She sing-songs the words the same as she always did when one of our close friends was attending dinner and she'd made them their favorites.

Beckett always thought it was over the top, while I only saw how much my mother cared about making others happy. I think that's why I grew into the woman I am. It was my mother and my desire to be just like her because it would make her proud.

His massive palm claps against his chest. "Mama Hughes, did you make those mashed red potatoes?"

"You know I did," she grins.

"I might never leave," Nash chuckles as his eyes meet mine again. "I can take that, Betty." He nods to the grocery bag still clutched to my chest with one hand, while I stare at the flowers in the other.

Had he known I've always loved multi-colored bouquets? Growing up obsessed with the stars, it was the closest I could get to the endless colors of the galaxies. I would pretend each flower was its own, full of stars and planets just waiting to be discovered. A whole universe that would carry me out of Cole County. Even then, I knew I wanted out.

But the Hugheses never leave, so I stayed.

The bag is suddenly pulled from my hand. Nash's brow scrunches as if in concentration when I flash him a glare. "I've got it." He ducks his head, quirking a corner grin before turning away from me.

Nash and my mother fall into a comfortable conversation about the rodeo and work. I pretend to be busy filling a vase and checking on the meatloaf in the oven. He's talked about his work over the years, but there's an openness that comes over him when he gets to chatting with my momma. So, I listen. I absorb every word, grinning like a fool, realizing how accomplished he's become.

Like so many others, Nash got far away from Cole County for college. Yet, he is one of the few who never came back. From the inflection in his tone, he sounds as if he is happy with his life. He enjoys Montana, and returning to Cole County is more of a chore than a choice.

Something about his honesty on the topic stabs me in the heart. I know I promised myself I was letting him go, but it hurts that he doesn't want to be here with all of us.

You're supposed to be letting go of this silly crush, Betty. That's all it was. I was never really in love with Nash Donovan. It was infatuation and nothing more. *Remember that when he flashes those blue eyes at you again*, I scold myself.

Watching him here in my kitchen, laughing with my mom like he belongs here, my mind is forgetting the promise we made to my heart. It's too easy to picture holidays spent the same way and random nights filled with family and laughter.

"Nash! You made it," Beckett bursts into the kitchen with our two golden retrievers on his heels.

My body involuntarily jumps, my back smacking into the full vase I just put on the counter, knocking it into the sink, where it shatters.

"Beatrice," my mother scolds. "What in the dickens has gotten into you?"

"Nothing, I—" Groaning, I reach into the sink, grabbing the flowers, eager to at least save those.

"Hey," Nash cages me in, his arms wrapping around me, pulling me back. The heat of his body sears my skin. *Holy hell,*

Nash Donovan is holding me. "You'll cut yourself," he warns, his tone so low it almost sounds like a growl.

"I-I can do it."

"Maybe you should just go set the silverware, Betty Minor," my mother chuckles. I roll my eyes, annoyed Mom would use the nickname they've called me since I was a child, and they'd find me sitting outside staring up at the stars.

Ursa Minor had always been my favorite constellation. The little bear sits up there next to its mama. Although they were always near each other, they became part of the enormous night sky and saw the world together. There was a time when I'd hoped Mom would have wanted to see the world with me, but we never did. She had no interest in traveling the way I've always wanted to.

There was too much to do around the farm, and she was always giving so much of her time to the youth in schools, at church, and even on the sports teams. My mother has always been everyone's mom; that's why they call her Mama Hughes.

Carefully placing silverware and napkins at each of our seats, I pause when I get to the chair Nash has always sat in—the seat to my right. I never questioned why he chose that one the first time he came over instead of sitting beside Beckett. And now I hope he doesn't sit beside me, because having him so close only breaks my heart.

The savory scent of fresh meatloaf out of the oven wafts up my nose. Every herb causes me to salivate. Nash, Beckett, and my mother come funneling into the dining room, each cradling piping-hot dishes with oven mitts.

"Betty, go wash up and grab your father," my mom croons, inhaling deep as she places freshly baked rolls on the table.

"Sure," I nod, tapping the back of my chair.

Moving past Nash, his scent mixes with my mother's cooking, causing my stomach to tighten against the urge to inhale like a weirdo.

My steps falter when I think I hear him whisper under his breath. "Hurry back, Beatrice."

Dammit, I can't do this.

CHAPTER 7

NASH

Home-cooked meals together at the dinner table weren't something we did in my house growing up. I've never held it against my parents. They were busy with the roughstock, and my sisters, Magnolia and Savannah, wanted nothing to do with ranch life. They spent more time at friends' houses than they did at home, and my parents never said a word. Neither did I. All their pop music and hordes of makeup drove me crazy. They became the exact type of women I have always stayed away from, preoccupied with their looks and more obsessed with being Pilates-thin than enjoying a good steak straight from the farm. Yet, despite my sisters being shallow, they were brilliant.

Still, I keep as close to them as they allow. They both left for New York City when they went to college. Obsessed with city life and not smelling like horseshit, they never looked back. I went to visit them once and swore I was never going back to that godforsaken city again. They found their place, and the ranch has always been mine.

I'll never understand how they settled into that life when they grew up in near-silence. There's nothing but noise, cars, and lights. You don't see any stars out there. There's never any quiet. My sisters may have complained about the smell out here, but that city stank like sewage.

Since they were two and three years older than me, I was alone once they left. I got used to eating at the table by myself. Mom always had the food prepared, but it seemed she and Pop always ate at different times. Not to mention, I was involved in sports year-round. It was my ticket out of here, too.

Then, in senior year, I took Beckett under my wing. I could tell from the moment he stepped foot on the football field that he had talent. He just needed refining, like anyone. So as captain, I did what anyone would do and privately coached him. It developed into a genuine friendship, which often led to sleepovers at the Hughes home and Sunday night dinners.

I hadn't realized how much I missed them until I left for college. I'd sit in the dining hall on Sunday nights, usually with friends, but I'd pretend it was the Hughes family there with me. When I met Katherine, she thought it was the most endearing thing, so she made a point of having dinner with me as much as our schedules allowed. It became the glue of our friendship before it developed into something more.

Still, the moment I crossed the Cole County line to come home, this house was the first place I stopped. Then Beckett graduated, and he too left for college. Though he didn't go far, I felt like an intruder continuing to show up for Sunday night dinners when he wasn't there anymore.

Now and then, I would if Mr. Hughes ran into me in town or Mama Hughes called me out of the blue, knowing it was a rodeo weekend. She knew my parents had always planned for me to take over the distribution business once my father retired. Until that day, I was free to do whatever I wanted.

There were countless times Mama Hughes and Katherine asked me how I felt about it. I never had an answer. I felt nothing at all. It was the plan. The expectation. What was there to feel? All I knew was it would bring me back here eventually, but until then, Montana became home.

And now I'm sitting here in the Hughes dining room, with Betty laughing loudly beside me, questioning whether any-where but here could be home. My gaze once again tracks down to the expanse of her thigh, exposed in that sundress with its delicate lace trim, which reminds me of lingerie. Each time she jerks forward, cupping her hand over her mouth to stifle her laughter, it hikes just a fraction higher.

She'd been so shocked when I said the flowers were for her, as if I'd made up the lie on the spot. It was the truth. I knew she'd be here, so I brought her flowers. I wasn't sure they were her favorites, but I remembered the times when I'd be here and she would be out in the garden, picking flowers of every color. They'd always end up on her dresser in her bedroom afterward, artistically blended as if she were creating her own rainbow.

When I first thought of the memory, I felt like such a dirty old man. I'd told myself I never looked at Betty as anything more than Beckett's little sister until she professed her "deep-seated love," but for a moment I questioned myself.

Had I looked at her as a teenager or seen her as anything more than a kid?

It wasn't until I realized I remembered everything about this place that my heart slowed and I could breathe again. I wasn't some gross pervert; I was simply reliving some of my happiest moments, which took place in this house.

I remembered it all after spending years within these walls. The rotation of hand rags Mama Hughes showcases, matching every season and holiday, each more cheesy than the last. The way Mr. Hughes always organized the remotes for the TV and his stereo system on the living room coffee table. Even the way Beckett alphabetized every award that hung on his wall. The third step at the front of the house has always sat at a slight angle. These countless details will live with me forever.

A grin tugs at the corner of my mouth, wondering if there's still a gouge in the wall in the mudroom that doubles as their laundry room. Beckett and I raced here after practice in our football gear when Mama Hughes told us she was cooking fried chicken for dinner. It was raining, but we bolted off the field, hopped in my truck in our gear, and booked it here. We were filthy, and she made us come through the mudroom, but Beckett almost fell over removing his shoulder pads and dented the wall. For months, he left a fleece hanging there, hoping his dad wouldn't notice, only for the guy to tell him he knew it was there the entire time.

I have just as many memories here as I do at my home.

"Do you remember that, Nash?" Beckett laughs.

The sound of my name pulls me out of my trip down Nostalgia Lane. "Sorry, food coma kicking in." I pat my stomach for good measure, as Mama Hughes *tsks* at me.

"Nonsense. You'll have another plate. I'm sure those washboard abs can handle it." Her wink makes Beckett groan, but I only chuckle, attempting not to blush when Betty quickly rakes her gaze from my face to my stomach, then away. If Mama Hughes weren't like a mother to me, I'd take offense, but never with her.

"Georgia," Mr. Hughes chides his wife as a flush creeps up over my cheeks. I've grown used to people making comments about my body. I'm the typical cowboy. All defined, rugged muscles built both out in the fields and at the gym. The sprinkle of gray in my beard—when I let it grow—and at my temples draws women to me like flies at a picnic. However, I've never been overly concerned with my appearance. It serves no purpose in my line of work.

"It's alright," I laugh. "They might hold up tonight, but I hear forties are no joke." The table bursts into laughter, Betty's eyes glistening with unshed tears as she continues to cackle and snort. A sound that should not be attractive, but shoots straight down to my cock. "What were you asking me, Beck?" I redirect the conversation.

"The time we had the team sleepover here, and we knew Case was a sleepwalker?" Beckett's face is bright red from his laughter as he tries to get the words out for what must be the second time.

"You leave that poor boy alone," Mama Hughes chuckles. "We found him out in the fields trying to ride the chickens."

Betty laughs louder, her palm pressed to her flat stomach as she curls forward. "Is that what happened? Dad said I had to stay in my room, so all I heard was the commotion of y'all trying to get him back inside the house."

Mr. Hughes grunts. "That's because that boy was out there in his underwear."

Betty only laughs louder, her hand cupped over her mouth as her face turns a shade of red that could only be found in a crayon box.

"Yeah, the guy had dreams of bull riding. He would try to ride random animals all the time," Beckett confirms.

Betty's nose scrunches as she straightens in her seat. "So weird."

The laughter finally dies down, and all five of us lean back in our chairs after Mama Hughes insists we eat massive bowls of peach cobbler and homemade vanilla bean ice cream.

"Beckett, why don't you boys go grab some drinks and sit out on the patio. It's a beautiful night," Mama Hughes croons, gathering several empty dishes in front of her and stacking them.

Draping an arm around her waist as she leans into him, he kisses her temple. The gesture is so tender, so familiar, as if it's second nature. They've always been like this. I used to think maybe Katherine and I would be too, but we were more likely to punch one another in the shoulder than share a heartfelt moment. "My wife is a genius," Mr. Hughes sighs.

Beckett disappears into the kitchen, wandering back out with three beers moments later. "Let's go, Nash."

"Actually, Mama Hughes, why don't you take my spot. I'll get these dishes cleaned and the food put away with Betty," I volunteer with a wide grin.

There's no missing Betty's sharp intake of air at my suggestion, those toned sun-kissed thighs pressing together as she forces a smile. Her hands knot in her lap before she places her palms on the table, shoving out of her seat awkwardly. The scent of her light perfume drifts my way, and I try my hardest not to inhale deeply like a fucking creep, but I can't help it. She smells like the river or the ocean after it's just rained. It's my favorite scent.

Before I can stand to help, she's gathered a stack of dishes and glasses in her hands and is already shuffling off to the kitchen.

For a woman who's supposedly in love with me, she acts like she can't wait to get away from me fast enough. I told her that nothing had to change, that I wouldn't treat her any differently, and I haven't, though I want to.

I've found myself wondering more often how her lips would taste and what her skin might feel like if I could touch her anywhere I wanted. Would that tan hue turn pink under my palm? Is she the type to purposely disobey her man, or would she follow every command with a "yes, sir" as those big doe eyes focused on my face?

The fantasies I've had about that woman would make most blush. *Fuck*, my cock twitches just thinking about it, forcing me to adjust myself beneath the table. Shoving out of my seat, I grab the bowl of mashed potatoes and our plates, stacking them.

"It's okay," she breathes, returning from the kitchen for the next load, her hand stretching out as if she were going to touch my arm, only to pull it back. "I can do it myself."

Grabbing my glass, my gaze meets hers. "Just do as I say."

Heat blazes in her stare, the most beautiful dark pink flooding her cheeks. Yet her mouth purses as she slowly gathers what's left on the table and disappears into the kitchen without another word.

Tonight might fucking kill me.

No, Nash. She will.

CHAPTER 8

BETTY

The second pile of dishes clangs into the sink, each one cleared of its remnants of food, after the leftovers were sectioned into the glass containers I bought my parents for Christmas. My mother was still using those plastic ones that eventually melt in the dishwasher and microwave, and I was tired of them.

Nash stops beside me as I grab the bottle of dish soap, sprinkling far more than necessary. Slamming the bottle down with enough force bubbles shoot out into the air, there's no one to be upset with but myself.

Turning the water to scalding, I'm determined to ignore the man hovering at my side until the baritone of his voice washes over me. "I'll wash, you dry," he says, his arm brushing mine.

Was that on purpose?

I swear I can't breathe. The air literally will not filter into my lungs as goosebumps break out over my skin from that slight touch.

It's ridiculous that I am so affected by him. He made it clear that no matter how I felt about him, nothing was happening between us. It's up to me to accept that. No one wants to be the pathetic woman pining over a man who couldn't give two shits about her. It was fine when he didn't know. I could pretend that someday might happen as much as I wanted. Now it's just pathetic to hang on.

I've never been that woman. I've left men for not treating me as I deserved in a heartbeat. Nash is the only one who has ever had this hold on me, and he doesn't even realize it. He doesn't understand. Maybe he doesn't care.

I swore to myself that I was not going to linger on my ridiculous fantasies anymore. You don't go and reject me and pretend like nothing happened. This isn't a movie where, if I wait around long enough, he'll realize what he's missing and come begging for my heart.

"You can put the leftovers in the fridge. They should be cool enough," I direct him. Anything, so I can't feel his breath on my skin or the heat radiating off his body as he hovers beside me.

"Betty."

My fingers curl over the sink edge as the water runs, the bubbles rising higher with each passing second. Pressing my eyes shut, I try to block it all out. He can't say my name like that, like he has something important to say and is begging for me to listen. He can't say my name with such tenderness. My mind might be made up, but my body and heart haven't caught up yet. They're still in Nash Land waiting to get on the ride.

"Please, don't."

"What did I do?" he questions, his fingers curling around my bare arm.

I'm ready to shake him off when the crack of the back screen door closing confirms we're in here alone. I can hear Beckett and our parents out there laughing before Mom turns on her stereo, which only plays 90s country music. It's been the same rotation of songs our whole lives.

I can't think when he's this close to me, when he's touching me. Not when his spicy pine scent is wafting up my nostrils and his warm breath is fanning across my cheek.

Before I can gather my thoughts, he shuts off the water, tugging my hand and pulling me behind him. "Nash, what are you—" I can't get the words out as he leads us down the hallway and straight to my childhood room, shutting us in and locking the door.

He spins me so fast my heart races, as my back presses against the door. His body hovers close to mine, the heat radiating off him as our chests seem to pump in unison. Large palms settle against the door beside my head, allowing him to angle his face over mine.

"I asked you a question, Beatrice?"

My throat is so dry I can barely swallow as I stare up into his cobalt eyes that seem darker than usual. His jaw works, the muscles twitching like a taut rope ready to snap. "I-um-I don't... What question?" It's a stumble through the words, my brain malfunctioning. Having the man of my dreams so close to me in my bedroom is overwhelming. A room I used to fantasize about him sneaking into in the middle of the night to hold me while we slept.

He dips his face to within an inch of mine, licking his lips as his gaze trails down to my mouth. Instinctively, I lick mine too, as if that will add moisture to my desert-dry mouth. "I asked you what I did? You've been avoiding me, acting like you can't wait to get away from me."

"Because I can't," I stammer once again, licking my lips.

His breath fans over my face as he tilts his head to the side, his hand brushing my hair out of the way before his lips brush the side of my neck. My fists clench at my sides, my eyes pressing closed so tightly it hurts. Nash Donovan's lips just touched me. They. Touched. Me.

He moans, flicking the tip of his tongue over the spot he just touched, the vibration moving through his chest and into mine as he leans in just a little closer. Close enough that with every heavy breath, my embarrassingly erect nipples brush against him.

"Nash, I—" It's meant to be a protest as his soft lips actually press to my skin, but it's a fail.

"Why can't you?" he purrs against my skin, his other hand finding my waist and squeezing.

Good God, I've wanted this since I could remember. I've wanted his hands on me and lips on my skin. There are whole dream sequences with that deep voice making my core tighten in anticipation. He could have given me that when I spilled my guts, but he didn't. Maybe that's partially my fault for avoiding him, but it's not like he chased after me either. However, that is what he's doing now. Sort of.

"Beatrice, I'm waiting. Answer me." He kisses my neck again, my head tilting to give him better access as his hand slips into my hair.

"Because you don't want me," I whisper.

His hands immediately drop from my body, his mouth pulling away from my bare skin as his eyes meet mine. Lust burns bright, causing the blues to swirl, but all I can feel is the cold of his lost touch. I want his hands back on me and his mouth on mine.

As if he heard my thoughts, he grabs my hand, slamming my palm over his crotch. *Fuck me and all things that are unholy.* He's huge and hard as a rock. "Tell me, Betty, does that feel like I don't want you?"

My mouth opens and closes several times trying to find the words, but I can't as his hand squeezes around mine, forcing me to grip him through his jeans. I'm on fire as he holds me there, neither of us willing to look away.

I did this to him. He's hard because of me. My mind goes fuzzy, my body acting before it can catch up and tell me this is the worst idea. Yanking him to me, one hand fisting his shirt at the center of his chest and the other rubbing his bulging cock through his pants, I do what I've always wanted.

I'm not bold like this. I'm not a prude, but I'm so fucking hot right now I don't know what else to do but crash my mouth to Nash's. He immediately opens up for me, his tongue swiping into my mouth. Releasing my hand, his slips back into my hair while the other grabs my ass, backing me into the door.

The length of his body presses against mine as he consumes me. No one has ever kissed me like this. No one has ever owned my mind and body simultaneously, making me think that without them, I would cease to exist. And for a second, I hate myself for caving. I was supposed to be steering clear. For all I know, this is nothing more than a joke to Nash. I could be just a warm body to pass the time.

I'm on the verge of coming to my senses when he sucks on my tongue, his palm slipping beneath my dress and squeezing my naked butt cheek. I'm not a big woman, but my ass is, and those cheeky underwear I love so much don't cover much.

"Fuck, baby," Nash groans into my mouth. "Keep rubbing me like that and I'm going to come in my jeans."

I only giggle against his mouth, sinking my fingers into the hair at the nape of his neck, crushing his mouth to mine. I'm lost in the deepening, hungry kiss, ready to give him anything he wants, just as his fingers dip into the front of my panties, and a knock cracks at my door.

My body jumps, stumbling and landing on my ass as Beckett's voice comes through the door, and the handle jiggles. "Betty?" he calls out. "You in there?"

"Uh," I pant, my eyes wide as I stare back at Nash, who looks like he has a cross between murder and regret in his eyes. "Uh, yeah. I got my dress wet doing the dishes. Just drying off a little."

"You're such a klutz," Beckett laughs. "Hurry up, Mom and Dad want to hang out with all of us before Nash has to leave."

"Yeah, okay. Yeah, I'm coming."

I wait until I hear Beckett's heavy footsteps down the hall before trying to get up, only for Nash to extend his hand, pulling me to my feet in one swift motion.

"You okay?" he questions, and I know whatever just happened has passed. He's put his guard back up, and I feel like a fool.

"I'm fine. I need to go finish the dishes." His hand finds my forearm, but I can't look at him. "Don't worry, I won't say anything or expect anything." My voice cracks, and I want to curl up and die because of it. How many times will I keep doing this to myself?

"Beatrice, I—"

"Please stop calling me that."

"Sorry-I." He clears his throat, releasing me before unlocking my bedroom door and grabbing the handle. The expanse of his back is all I can see, but I hear his words loud and clear. "That can't happen again." Then he walks out, and I crumple back to the floor.

Dammit, Betty.

CHAPTER 9

NASH

G runts and the clank of weights hitting the rack fill the gym. It was the only place that could help after this past weekend.

Vortex Fitness became my happy place a long time ago. The national chains and gimmicky training facilities don't do it for me. I needed black walls, solid equipment, and the scent of sweat. I needed a place where patrons were more concerned with pushing their bodies to the limit than with creating content for social media.

It's the only place where the noise can drown out my thoughts, other than the family ranch. I'd meant to create my own on my property. That's why I bought the fifty acres, but life got away from me, and Katherine was never interested while we were together. So I kept my head down and focused on everyone else, ignoring my need for a piece of home here in Montana.

Pain lances through my jaw as I grit my teeth, raising my weights for a fifth set I have no business trying to crank out. My muscles shake as I drive the hundred-pound dumbbells up at an angle for what feels like the millionth time. Every fiber burns as if live flames engulf my tissues, but it doesn't compare to the images and sounds of Betty that will forever live in my mind.

I can't get her out of my fucking head, and I need to. *But that kiss. Her whimper. The brush of arousal on my fingertips... Fuck...*

Pushing out another rep, I fight my thoughts, not wanting to get hard in the gym with a bunch of massive dudes and the no-nonsense women that will beat your ass, though they're half your size. Sweat pours down my face, over the bridge of my straight nose to my mouth, where each forceful exhale sends droplets flying.

Hunt chuckles, "Save some for tomorrow." Slapping my shoulder, the ache seems to throb down my arm as he rounds the bench I've been perched on.

"Don't you have your own workout to do?" I snarl, struggling through yet another thrust of my arms up and out.

He quirks a blond brow, his hazel eyes sparkling with that knowing stare. "I'm done, and we have a meeting in an hour and twenty-seven minutes."

The guy has a sense of humor like no other and will call you on every bit of your shit, but with business, he's the best partner a guy could ask for. He's meticulous. No detail is ever missed. Hunt is the glue every business needs.

With a huff, my elbows bend, my arms violently shaking as I fight to press out one last rep. "Alright, that's enough," he groans, his hands pressing behind my elbows to extension and then supporting some of the weight as they sink back toward my chest.

He doesn't say a word, returning the weights to the rack and then waiting for me to shove off the bench.

My head is no clearer as we grab our bags from the locker room and head toward our separate vehicles. "I'll be by in twenty," he calls over his shoulder before climbing into a tiny ass sports car. My lip curls, praying he shows up in his SUV instead; otherwise, we're taking my truck. No way I'm folding my large frame into that tin can again.

Unlike me, Hunt enjoys the flash of nice things. He grew up in a typical middle-class family, but has always had an eye for the finer things. But he's never had a thing handed to him. He attended college on an academic scholarship and had most of his graduate school paid for with money he saved from working and a start-up he and a business school friend developed, which they later sold.

He did what any business graduate would do: he went into corporate America, working his way up to a high-paying director's job, and hated every minute. My friend likes nice things, but no one knows how to manage money better than he does and then make it grow. He's been smart with every cent he's made, which made it that much easier to bring him on as my partner.

I drive home in silence. Sometimes it's the only way I can clear my head. But once again, I can't. Not when all I can think about is how wet Betty was when I sank my fingers into her panties. I'd wanted to take her right there, hold her against the door with my forearm, with her ass high in the air, begging me to mark her skin.

"Dammit, Nash," I scold myself.

It's a ten-minute drive toward the mountains before I hit my mile-long driveway, the path curving upward until it levels out at the top of the hill, revealing my black and gray home. The exterior is modern and square with hints of farmhouse in the exposed wood detailing. It's what Katherine wanted.

It's just a house. A massive house that's devoid of any feeling or the touches that make it a home. The realization that it's not like the Hughes home hits me like a freight train to the gut. Funny, it's not like mine either, littered with pictures of us kids growing up and the many moments of Pop traveling to rodeos.

Cutting the engine, I'm quick to hop out of my truck, my legs wobbling, barely able to support my weight after that forty-minute sprint—something I've never done.

It's a shuffle through the motions as I make my way up to my bedroom and into the master bathroom. I make quick work of hopping into the shower, scrubbing my body clean, and then allowing myself five minutes to stand under the spray. Five minutes of my forehead resting on the cold marble. Five minutes to put Betty out of my mind and not fist my cock until I come all over my shower wall.

Five minutes pass far too quickly.

I'm just walking out the front door, dressed in my typical dark-wash jeans, button-up, and suit jacket with my cowboy boots, as Hunt stops at the top of the drive. A relieved sigh leaves me as I spot his Range Rover idling, its music cranked loud enough that I can hear every word, even with the window rolled up.

Climbing into the passenger side, he hands me a tablet with the account already pulled up. I'm quick to turn down the volume, eyeing his custom-made suit. Like me, Hunt has the build of a football player. We're both tall, with a decent amount of girth that fills out our clothes. He claims his muscles are so large that off-the-rack suits don't fit, but I order all my jackets online or in-store, and I also bought my only tuxedo in a store.

His money, his choice.

"They're losing a ton of money doing this sale," I mumble.

"That's what I've been telling the old man, but they're adamant that they need to get rid of the land and livestock," Hunt relays with a distant hum.

"The urgency is just... off. It's a well-run dairy farm, one of the biggest in the state. Why wouldn't they want to at least get paid what it's worth?" I wonder aloud.

"Beats me," Hunt answers, flying down the back road that will take us to Blumsberry Farm.

We're silent for a while as I review the numbers for the hundredth time. We've been trying to convince the family that they can do better, which should have been easy to see, as they've had numerous other offers, including one that was significantly over the asking price. It's my job to guide them in evaluating the offers and making the right deal, but I refuse to force anyone into a contract they don't want.

"So, are you going to tell me what this morning was about?" Hunt asks, expertly navigating the weaving curves at a speed too fast to be considered safe. But that's my fault. I made us late.

"I needed a good sweat, that's all."

"Bullshit. What happened at home that got you so worked up? Were your sisters there or something?" He chuckles, knowing it's always a joyous event when those two make their way back to Cole County with their husbands and children in tow. They've both been married for eighteen years, and both have three children; their eldest are sixteen and fifteen. Those two have always acted like they were twins, perhaps because they were born only a year and two months apart. It's like they planned their whole lives together. They even live in the same damn neighborhood.

"No. I haven't seen them since Christmas," I groan, recalling how heinous that had been. They acted as if they were too good to come back to the ranch, choosing instead to stay at the luxury hotel in Carruthersville rather than at our family home. The only reason I was looking forward to it was to hang out with my nieces and nephews. I've always loved kids. Even as a young man, I knew I always wanted some of my own, but some things aren't in the cards for some of us.

My mind immediately jumps to Betty and how good it would feel to move inside her bare before filling her pretty pussy with my cum. I'd make sure she kept every drop. How else would she get...

"Fuck!" I bark out loud, tossing the tablet on the backseat, only for Hunt to stare at me as if I've lost my mind.

"So..." he stretches out the word, and I finally cave.

"Do you remember Beck? The kid from back home I used to play football with in college?" I groan, scrubbing my hands over my face as if that will clear the image of Betty naked out of my head.

"Yeah, of course, but why?" Confusion knits his brow as he turns onto the road that will lead us to the main drive of the farm.

"Uh, so last fall his younger sister told me she has a... crush on me. I kind of brushed it off, but then I started thinking about her—"

"Hold the fuck up," he interrupts. "The girl who liked to sit outside in the middle of the night?"

I groan, hating that I described her that way now, but it's how I remembered her best, always staring up at the stars. "Yeah. I kissed her, and fuck, all I can think about is how I passed up on fucking her until she couldn't stand or say her name."

"Uh..." Hunt hums.

"Yeah, I fucked up. I told her it wouldn't happen again, but I still can't get her out of my head." Each word is a snarl through gritted teeth. I'm not sure if I'm angrier at her for blowing this door wide open, which I'd never considered, or at myself for wanting it.

"So, what's the problem?" Hunt questions.

The problem? There are so many. I'm eight years her senior and good friends with her older brother. Her family has always treated me as if I were their own. I'm damaged goods after my divorce, though neither of us was at fault. But worst of all, Betty is the type of woman who wants things I never dreamed about and a life I can never provide.

She'll want the white picket fence and a husband who's always around. She'll need a man who can commit himself to Cole County year-round, and I'm not that. Women like that want a kind man to make love to them in the bedroom, nestled in their bed. I want to bend her over every surface, including the bed of my truck, and fuck her until she sees those stars she holds so precious.

"I'm not what she really wants," I nearly whisper, training my gaze outside the window just as Hunt pulls his SUV to a stop.

Betty thinks she wants me, that she wants this, but as soon as she gets to know me, she'll realize that she never honestly could.

CHAPTER 10

BETTY

A groan leaves me as I shuffle into my apartment. It had been a long day at the Miller house. A pipe burst, then we had to bring in someone to clear up the water, followed by removing the furniture in one of the bedrooms, which is going to screw with the reservations we already have for next week. Only for us to later realize the water had leaked down onto the living room furniture, too.

This was horrible timing. There's a junior competition being held at the ranch next weekend, and we're booked.

I hadn't even known about it until Gray found me a few days ago. For a minute, I convinced myself I was hallucinating since I hadn't been sleeping. How could I when I finally had Nash's hands and mouth on me?

He'd been right there with me. Damn my brother for interrupting. Then again, maybe that was a blessing. If Nash had slept with me, he would have regretted it. The truth was there in his eyes before he walked out of my room and promptly left.

My mother said he'd gone through his goodbyes so quickly, claiming he had to get back to Montana for an emergency, that she hadn't even been able to stand up out of her chair.

Afterward, I couldn't face them, sure that my features revealed the heartbreak and shame. They would see that I was on the verge of tears, finally having something I'd wanted all my life, just to be rejected again when I knew better.

I. Knew. Better.

"Ouch!" I shout as my shin hits the bench by the front door.

The thing has been there since I moved in six years ago, yet I run into it today, when there's still enough light outside the living room windows to guide my way.

"Nice one, Betty," I chastise myself as I limp over to the couch.

A deep breath fills my nostrils as I try to ignore the ache in my leg. It's only seconds before my eyes flutter shut, relaxation uncoiling my sore muscles while I sink into the couch, before my phone vibrates in my bag.

With a huff, I pull the offending device free, bringing it to my ear on the third ring.

"Hello."

"Betty, hey," Jim sighs. "I need ya to come in tonight. Kellan called out again." My boss sounds so tired. Just as exhausted as I am, if not worse.

But I'm not supposed to be at the bar again until next week. My schedule went from daily to no more than a few times a week. I'd already put in my time on Monday and last night.

"There's no one else?" I ask.

Jim sighs loudly again. "Come on, Betty. You know you're the best I got."

My eyes press shut, breathing silently through my nose as my mouth pinches in resignation. "Right. Yeah. I'll be there in twenty."

"Thanks, kid."

He ends the call, and it takes everything in me not to break down and cry. But I'm a people pleaser. I have always been far too eager to keep everyone around me content. If it makes someone else happy, I do it. If you need me to be the life of your party, I'm there. Need help? No problem; Betty Hughes is on the way. It's why I've never left Cole County. No Hughes ever has, and I couldn't be the first. It would let my family down.

Shuffling toward the bedroom, I strip out of my clothes, pulling out a fresh pair of jeans and a denim vest as my top. Yanking my most comfortable cowboy boots out of the closet, I'm dressed in less than five minutes. Fortunately, I'd done my makeup today, so all I need is a little dry shampoo and I'm out the door.

At least I'll have my regulars to boost my mood.

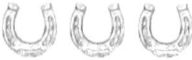

When I arrive, The Thirsty Pony is packed. Certain weeknights definitely draw a crowd during the warmer months, but never like this. Shoving through the crowd, for once, I don't recognize most of the faces. There must be something drawing in all the tourists.

"Thanks again," Jim darts from behind the bar, leaving me with a crowd eagerly waiting for their drinks.

Now is the time for fun Betty. She is the woman who smiles and occasionally shamelessly flirts back with the cowboys and wannabes who wander through here. She'll pretend to take a shot with you and slide your drink down the bar with a wink.

One after another, our patrons call out their orders. My hands and feet move faster than I would have expected with the exhaustion coursing through me. The rush giving me a second wind I hadn't thought was possible. A few women giggle as I hand them the fruity drinks they requested, which makes me gag just thinking about that overly sugary taste. Yet, it's the type of cocktail fun Betty would toast high in the air, causing the woman to nod my way when I pretend to agree it's the exact type of refreshing drink for spring. This is the Betty who is girly and enjoys dressing up, caking on enough makeup to hide every imperfection.

"We love your top," the petite blonde calls out over the music.

"Thanks," I wink.

"Your boobs look great!" her friend shouts, nodding as she drinks from her straw with her pinky out.

I fight not to roll my eyes. These were the types of girls I was friends with in high school. The same ones who thought I was like them in college, but I wasn't. I let my peers turn me into a fun, girly girl who was the life of the party, because back then, I didn't know any better. I needed to fit in like everyone else, because that's what makes everyone else happy.

My favorite line dance song comes over the speakers, my shoulders and hips swaying as I pop the tops on a line of beer bottles.

"Is one of those for me?" A male voice pulls my attention away from my task, my body going still as Ward stares back at me.

"No, but you can order one," I grin back at him. It'd be impossible not to with a face as handsome as his. Those hazel eyes sparkle in the dim light as he leans forward, flashing perfect white teeth. The tooth next to his left canine is slightly protruding; the imperfection is endearing. There's not a single one on Nash.

Betty, stop it!

Ward leans forward on the bar, his elbows digging into the wood as he clasps his hands in front of him. He says nothing as I distribute the drinks before pausing in front of him again. "How about instead of ordering a drink, I order a date with you?"

There's no hiding the flush that creeps up over my skin as he stares at me expectantly. "I-well," I let out a slow breath.

"I'm sorry," he says, raising his palms, patting the air. "You must have a man already. I didn't mean to overstep." He genuinely appears embarrassed by his behavior. Shifting as if he's going to slip off the barstool, I reach out and snatch his hand, holding him still.

"No. I mean." His eyes slowly meet mine, and it's as if he melts into my stare. No one has ever looked at me like that except... *No, Betty!* I promised myself I was letting go of this infatuation with Nash. I have to for my sake because at this point, it's just plain pathetic lusting after a man who regrets kissing you.

"No?" Ward questions, cocking a brow.

"I mean, no, I don't have a... man. I'm single, and I would love to go out with you." My cheeks flush all over again, our eyes locked until some asshole yells from the other end of the bar.

"Hey, if you're done eye fuckin' your man, can I get some service down here?"

The bright glow that had been in my eyes shifts to dark fury. I may be the bubbly girl with those I care about, but I don't take shit from people in my bar. Especially not some out-of-towner who thinks he's something special.

"Hey, buddy, you don't talk to a lady like that," Ward interjects.

I know he's trying to be sweet, but it only bugs me he's defending me. I'm no delicate flower. Working in a bar with a bunch of men who like to get shit-faced drunk, I had to learn to hold my own.

"I've got this." I place a hand on Ward's forearm before moving down to the other end of the bar, tossing a hand rag over my shoulder. "Apologize," I say calmly, staring down the stranger.

"How about you do your job?" he snaps, cackling with his buddies. "Get me a damn drink."

Turning on my heel, I walk away until the guy grabs my arm, yanking me back. I can keep my composure as long as the patrons don't get combative, but when they do, I lose my shit.

My back slams into the edge of the bar with the force of his strength. The guy laughs uncontrollably, thinking he has me, when I twist my body to the side, alleviating the pressure, only to quickly reach out with my other hand, grab his ratty hair, and slam his cheek down onto the bar top. He immediately lets me go, trying to fight against my hold. Grabbing hold of his wrist, twisting hard, a feminine yelp escapes him.

"You..." he starts.

"Don't finish that. I am going easy on you, so why don't you and your friends go find another bar? Hmm. I won't serve you, and if you're rude again, I'll make sure you're laid out on this floor," I snap through gritted teeth. "Now, are we going to have a good rest of the night?"

He grunts, trying to nod before I release him.

The guy is smart enough not to say a word as he and his friends stalk out of the bar. Their departure signals all the regulars to cheer and whistle. It's not the first time they've seen me handle things on my own. Beckett is the one who took self-defense classes so he could teach me to defend myself, knowing I was determined to stay at the bar. When I have the time, I still take them to stay sharp.

"Wow," Ward breathes. "Betty Hughes, I just might be in love with you."

At least someone is.

CHAPTER 11

BETTY

"That was exhausting," River collapses on the brand new living room couch that was just delivered to the Miller house.

"You didn't have to come help," I sigh, slumping next to her, allowing my arm to fall over the back of the couch.

"Yeah, well, Gray is out there with Tate, Reed, and Nash. Something about prepping the horses." River waves a hand as if it's too much for her to focus on.

I do my best not to sit a little straighter at the mention of Nash's name. I hadn't known he was going to be here this weekend, but I shouldn't be surprised. Gray had mentioned that he would be around more, now that he was taking over his father's distribution business and needed to attend rodeo events more often.

But this is a barrel racing competition only. The Donovan specialty is roughstock. It doesn't add up.

It's only then that I latch onto a name I don't recognize. I made it my mission when I took over Miller Inn to learn everyone's names and positions. If I were going to be their coworker and see them every day, I would want to address them properly. *Reed.* That one is new.

I suppose there may be a new hire I haven't reviewed yet. Funny thing is, when you brag to your boss that you memorized everyone's name and position, you automatically get additional responsibilities like maintaining personnel files. It was Tate asking, and he looked so exhausted, so I couldn't say no. Nor would I. Betty never says no. Betty is fun and compliant. She's helpful no matter the cost.

"Who is Reed?" I ask.

River scrunches her brow as if confused by my question. "The bullfighter? He's here every day working the ranch."

"Bullfighter?" My features scrunch, recalling their names. "James, Conrad, Maverick, and Whitaker. There are a few others that come and go, but those are the main four."

River slams the heel of her hand into her forehead. "Whitaker. Yeah, him. You don't call him Reed like everyone else?"

I hadn't. His file said Whitaker R. Lancaster. I'd met him shortly after construction started, and when I called him by name, he never corrected me. Every time I've seen him since, he hasn't said a thing, not even when I started calling him Whit for short. He's a pleasant guy, but keeps to himself. When he's not working the rodeo here, he competes in bullfighting competitions, which is insane.

My head shakes as I stretch out further, inhaling the scent of cloth straight from the factory. My couch had smelled the same when I bought it six years ago. That seems like a lifetime ago now. The three-cushion sofa was supposed to be a placeholder until I could find the courage to strike out on my own, beyond the Cole County line, but I never did. I stayed, just like we all do. "No, I've called him Whitaker or Whit since day one. He never said a thing."

"Odd," River shrugs before shifting to face me. "Anyhow, tell me about this date you have tonight."

A flush creeps up over my throat and onto my cheeks. Embarrassment floods my insides. I've been so busy the past few days that I haven't even thought about Ward or our date. But I hadn't thought about Nash either, so maybe that's a good sign.

"He's a calf roper new to the rodeo here. We met on opening weekend, and then he happened to be at the bar. That's all, really. I don't know anything about him."

"Do you want to know more about him?" River cocks a brow, resting her jaw on her fist.

My teeth sink into my lower lip as I worry the flesh. I know I want love and a relationship. River and Gray make my insides rage with jealousy. I thought I had that once until the unthinkable happened. Shoving the memories out of my mind, I focus on River's moss green eyes. The woman is absolutely stunning, with her warm brown skin, vibrant eyes, and wild, dark curls. She is the definition of exotic.

"I want what everyone wants. Yah know, to be happy and find their person..." My words trail off as my fingers twist in my lap.

"But..."

"But..." I echo her.

"You're still hung up on Nash?" I nod before she continues. "Betty, I know it's easier said than done, but if he's showing you he won't, then you should believe him. Y'all shared a passionate moment, and then he bolted. I think that's your answer."

"I was wondering where no-nonsense River was," I chuckle, trying to hide the tears burning behind my eyes.

I'd hoped Nash hadn't meant what he said when he walked out of my room. His eyes and body had said something entirely different. Hadn't they?

"Thanks to you and my sexy cowboy at home, I don't have to be that woman all the time anymore." There's a lightness to her tone, but her eyes give her away. River is as tough as they come. Choosing a male-dominated field as an orthopedic surgeon wasn't easy for her. She had to be better and constantly remind them that her talent matched or exceeded theirs.

Scooting over, I wrap River in a tight hug. We were never close in our younger years, but I am so grateful for her now. When I finally pull away, her hard stare is back. The moment has passed, and she once again has her armor in place. "You should go find that hot husband of yours and get outta here. He should be spending your day off ravaging you, not playing with those damn horses."

River glances down at her stomach, or maybe her lap, before standing and grabbing her purse from the brand new coffee table. "If your date goes bad, you call me. Gray will come get you."

"Thanks, but Beckett already offered first."

River snorts. "Your brother is something else. But he definitely knows how to protect the women he loves."

She's quick to leave the house, abandoning me to my thoughts. There had been a time when I thought River might end up with my brother for the long haul. I'd hoped for it, even though she was always this badass I looked up to. Not to mention a lawyer and a future doctor would be the ultimate power couple.

But in the end, Beckett loved her more than she ever would love him. I see it now. It was for the best. She moved on and built her own life in Kentucky before coming back here. There was a purpose in that. She found a piece of herself, then found

Gray and ultimately became the woman she was always meant to be.

She moved on, but my brother hasn't. That pained look still lives in his features whenever he sees her, and it's worse if Gray is there too. I want to tell him to get over it, but that would mean I needed to follow the same advice and leave Nash behind.

Resigned to do just that, I shove off the couch, shower, and pick out my favorite flirty spring dress.

This date is exactly what I need.

If you had asked me what I expected from Ward's date, I wouldn't have known what to tell you.

I've dated different types of men, and for the most part, the first date is a clone of the last: dinner, a movie, or a walk by the lake if the weather is nice. It becomes rote repetition, where you're counting the minutes waiting for it to end unless they're funny or intelligent enough to distract you with great conversation.

But Ward had other plans. Thirty minutes south in Sloth County, their spring fair was in full effect. When we arrived, I made assumptions that were once again wrong. I figured we'd grab some food, walk around, and watch him try to win me some stuffed animal I won't remember the origins of in a year. But he led me to the bumper cars.

"Up for a little competition?" He winks, flashing me that grin that makes my core tighten.

His hazel eyes glint with mischief, and I only nod, racing ahead of him and jumping into a blue car. He picks the one right beside me, and before I've even settled in, the battle begins.

Ward rams into me over and over, my laughter ringing out as my chestnut waves fly through the air from the impact. My cheeks burn and my belly aches. When was the last time I had this much fun? The type where there are no expectations but non-stop laughter and stories we'll tell later that won't make me blush in front of my parents.

As the ride ends, I'm still laughing in my car when Ward extends his hand, pulling me to my feet. "You're one tough opponent, Betty Hughes." He grins widely, that crooked tooth flashing my way as he weaves his fingers through mine. I let him, finding comfort in his warm, rough palm.

"You know, when I first asked you on this date, I wasn't thinking of this place," he says as we stroll hand-in-hand toward the games.

"And where were you going to take me?" I'm genuinely curious. Will he be like all the rest?

"There's a farm right outside the county lines where you can pick flowers—all different types and colors. You seemed like the kind of woman who likes bright colors," he almost whispers, nervously chuckling under his breath.

"Flower picking?" I gasp.

His brows lift before dropping as if in defeat. "Yeah," he croaks awkwardly, running his hand over the back of his head. "I thought you'd like pretty things, but not necessarily given to you. More like treasured and observed."

My feet stop as I turn to face him, a shy grin pulling at my lips. "I would have loved that date too," I whisper, before pressing up on my toes and kissing his cheek.

I'm on the verge of pulling away when his palm glides along my jaw, his thumb rubbing back and forth in soft strokes. "I really want to kiss you right now."

My lips part, a ragged breath pulled in as I watch him through my lashes. "I think I would love that too."

Soft, warm lips press to mine. The type of kiss that makes you melt into your lover's touch, eager to stretch the moment of connection. It's not hungry like Nash and I had been, but my insides still burn.

When he pulls away, I can only giggle. Swiping my thumb over his mouth, I wipe away my lipstick. "Better."

Ward says nothing more as he retakes my hand, leading us toward that hammer game made for guys who like to show off how much muscle they have.

"Okay, Betty. I watched you make a grown man cry. Let's see what else you've got."

CHAPTER 12

NASH

I've missed the stink of a day's worth of work on the ranch. There's a different sort of ache that lives in your muscles, as your shirt clings to sweat-drenched skin, smeared with dirt.

Originally, I'd planned to be in Montana for another week before returning to Cole County. A week away from knowing Betty was right there, believing I didn't want her. I do; I just can't. I shouldn't.

Pop is the reason I'm out here in the field, with my t-shirt hanging out of my back pocket, and sweat droplets burning my eyes. Apparently, the promotion hosting this junior barrel race competition was requesting a few pickup and patrol horses. Per usual, Pop volunteered. It made no sense to me. We've never supplied horses for that sort of thing, but my father is the type to solve a problem if he has the resources.

Gray mentioned they were short a few guys this week and needed an extra hand. It wasn't a question of whether I would help or not. It's always a yes if I'm available. We all grew up here at Boulder Ranch, in a way, so it's only natural to want to keep it alive. So here I am, throwing hay bales.

Too bad Gray bailed the moment he saw River. I can't blame him. The guy is fucking glowing being married to that gorgeous woman. He and Tate have been through a lot of shit over the years. They both deserve the happiness they've found.

The timing worked out well since I'd just closed another deal, and Hunt could handle the others that were pending. Choosing to count this as a blessing instead of a curse, I've worked at Boulder and our home ranch during the day and spent the evenings with my parents the past few nights. They're getting older, and time waits for no one. A thought that seems to hit at the worst time, as Betty's laugh punches me in the gut.

Every breath comes in a heaving pant as I drag myself back up to the Miller house. I should have stayed at my own, but why not torture myself knowing I'm feet away from the one woman I refuse to have.

My head snaps up, and there she is. Her laughter rings out through the humid spring air as her head falls back, my cock twitching at the sight. I'm so exhausted there's no way my old ass should be able to get hard right now.

The man she's with grips her waist, helping her keep her balance as her feet cross one in front of the other, fighting to control her cackle.

Whatever he said can't be that damn funny.

The guy stops at the door, his hand finding that same hip I'd held a week ago. Then his lips touch the same mouth I'd devoured. Betty leans into him, giggling before they pull apart and she slips inside.

What the fuck? A week ago, she was all over me. She was mine. Who the hell is this asshole moving in on my...

Stop that, Nash. She's not yours. You made that clear.

A million emotions course through me as he stands at the door as if waiting for her to open it again, only to knock. I hold my breath, hoping she doesn't. *Please don't open it, baby. Fuck!*

My breath lodges in my lungs as I hold it in, hoping she leaves him out here when we might only be minutes from a storm. Yet, the door creaks open, her face appearing around the edge as she smiles brightly at him. Will she ever smile at me like that again?

Inching closer, it's a strain to hear the words exchanged, but I don't miss the glow of happiness that never leaves her face. Or his deep laughter as she takes his hand and pulls him inside.

I'm barely thinking as I storm toward the house, my shirt balled in my fist. Punching in the code, the door clicks open, and Betty's laughter drifts from the kitchen.

There's no stamping down my emotions as I march in that direction. My head is screaming that some other man has his hands on my woman. *My woman?* Betty isn't mine. Yet I can't stop what's about to happen.

Clearing my throat, Betty jumps away from the man who just had his arms around her waist and his tongue down her throat.

"Nash. I... What are you doing here?" Her eyes are wide as they rake over my naked torso, the dirt and sweat still clinging to my skin. I'm not a territorial man. Jealousy isn't part of my makeup, and I don't flex like I'm hot shit to impress a woman. I never have, yet here I am in the kitchen of the Miller house, making sure every muscle pops with my molars painfully grinding, witnessing another man's hands on that woman.

"I'm helping out for the weekend. Tate said I could stay here at the house," I explain calmly.

"Oh, well. Tate's wrong. The rooms are all full. We're down one after the pipe break earlier this week." She takes a step closer to the guy whose face I am just starting to place. Some nobody calf roper that's new to the Boulder circuit.

Taking a step closer, my palms rest on the island. The surface is spotless except for the two tumblers sitting in front of them. "Tate offered the couch; I already know about the room. And who are you?" I cock my chin toward the man who still dares to touch what's mine.

"Oh, I'm sorry," Betty apologizes, stepping out of his hold, but guiding him around the island. "I assumed y'all would have met. Nash, this is Ward Ferrell."

He sticks out his hand to shake mine, my grip tighter than necessary as I keep my eyes focused on his face. "And you are?" I ask again.

His smile is warm and inviting as he releases my hand. "I, well. I competed here opening weekend. That's how I met Betty here." His arm drapes around her shoulder, his fingers rubbing idly.

When he'd touched her before, she'd leaned into him. She welcomed his hands on her skin, but now she's stiff as if she can't decide if she should or not. It reminds me of when my sisters started dating and bringing boys home. Magnolia was always unsure if it was okay to share a kiss or hold hands, while Savannah didn't give a shit. She'd sit on the guy's lap while my dad stared daggers at them, and the guy sweated so much he left a spot on the couch.

Before I can respond, the guy continues. "A good friend of mine's daughter is competing this weekend, so I booked one of the cabins. It was the perfect opportunity to take Betty on our first date, too." There's not an ounce of smugness in the guy. He's genuinely excited that he got to spend time with her. And by the glint in his eyes, he's hoping there will be a second.

"Hope you two had fun, but I need a shower and some sleep," I all but growl.

"You can have my room again," Betty chirps. The high-pitched tone of her voice is fabricated. Forced happiness so she can pretend she's fine. This guy wouldn't notice it, but I've known her for most of her life.

"Are you two leaving?" I hate that I'm fucking standing here giving them the third degree, like I'm not a grown man with some fucking self-control. My molars grind, and the muscles in my jaw flex so hard I want to cry out. I have no right to stand here and make them feel uncomfortable or act as if I have any claim to Betty when I don't.

They're both silent before Ward finally takes the hint. "I promised my buddy I'd meet him early for breakfast. I should go."

"I'll walk you to the door," Betty volunteers, slipping her arm around his and leading him the opposite direction from me around the island.

I watch them move the short distance to the door, where I have to listen to the sound of him kissing the mouth that should be on mine.

The sound of the door closing lifts my spirits. It's just her and me, and now we can have a chat. A conversation I have no business starting if I'm not going to follow through. I don't understand why I am so upset at seeing her with someone else.

Betty. Is. Not. Mine.

The word "yet" floats through my mind, and I have to swat it away. *Fuck, what is happening to me?*

The clap of her bare feet on the hardwood almost makes me turn around, until she grabs my wrist, leading me down the hall to her bedroom, slamming the door behind us. "What the hell was that, Nash?"

I've never seen Betty angry. I've never seen her as anything but fun-loving, smiling Betty. She's the woman everyone wants to be friends with. The woman who never says no if someone needs help. She's the life of the party and everyone's best friend after a single interaction.

That's not the Betty standing in front of me. Her nostrils flare with her barely contained frustration as her face turns a shade of red that wouldn't even be healthy for a tomato.

"I just wanted to get some sleep, and you were seconds from fucking that guy in the kitchen." It's the wrong thing to say. I know that the moment the words pass my lips. I'm not an asshole, especially not to her or any other woman. Yet the words spewed free as the green monster of jealousy took over.

She rears back as if slapped, before a glassy sheen settles over her eyes. *Fuck, no.* If she cries, I will lose it. "Is that what you think of me?" Her words are watery as she holds back tears. Her voice is so broken that I immediately hate myself.

"No, I don't. I'm sorry, Betty." Reaching for her, she quickly steps back, sorrow tugging at her gorgeous features. *Please don't cry, baby.* "I'm just tired, but that's not an excuse for speaking to you that way."

"What did I ever see in you?" she whimpers. "All these years, I thought you were nothing but a kind man. I thought you cared about the people in your life, but you don't. Not after... not after last week and the way you just spoke to me. I'm not a kid anymore, so you can't charge in here and tell me what to do. You made it clear you could never want me." Her hands run down her body as if reminding me she's standing right there. "I've wasted years pining over you, and for what?"

The first tear finally breaks free, and I can't help myself. Cupping the side of her face, I wipe it away with my thumb. "Andromeda, I'm sorry."

Her eyes flare at the nickname. I used to call her that as a kid. It was her favorite galaxy. She said she was just like the Andromeda constellation. I never considered what she meant by that back then, but now I do.

"You remembered?" she breathes, finally melting into my touch.

"I'm going to level with you, and I need you not to hate me for it." Her breath quickens as she tries to pull away from me, but I grab hold of her hip, pulling her body flush against mine.

My cock swells in my jeans, but I don't hide it. Instead, I hold her tight to me so she can feel me when I say this.

"Nash, if you're..."

"I'm talking. You're going to listen." She nods. "I think it's pretty clear I am attracted to you. My cock is so hard right now, the fucker hurts enough to bring me to my knees. I think we both know that what happened a week ago would have been a mistake if I'd taken it further." Once again, she tries to pull away. "Stop trying to run from me." Her glassy eyes meet mine as her mouth presses into a straight line. Lowering my face to hers, I'm so close that a flick of my tongue would allow me a taste of her. "I am a man with particular needs. Needs that don't align with what you need."

"And tell me, how do you know what I need?" Those soft lips brush over mine as she speaks.

And, fuck, I once again can't control myself, dipping my head to capture her mouth with mine. It doesn't matter that she had another man's mouth on hers ten minutes ago. I needed to taste her. Betty is what I imagine sunshine would taste like, or an explosion of twinkling stars in the sky. It's consuming and addictive.

Her short nails scrape over my scalp as she deepens the kiss, her moan vibrating down my throat. I'm a crazed man when her skin is on mine. There's no control or telling myself to stop. Gripping her under her ass, her legs immediately wrap around my waist before my free arm clears everything on the six-drawer dresser, and I drop her there.

Her grin stretches across my mouth, but she doesn't break contact as her hands dig into my hair and her pussy grinds against my throbbing dick.

"Are you wet for me again?"

"If you want to know, you should check for yourself," she breathes, tugging at the back of my head. But I resist, dipping down in front of her, while pushing her dress up her toned thighs.

"You're beautiful," I mumble, placing wet kisses up the inside of her thigh, before my nose drags along the crotch of her panties.

"Nash, you can't."

"I can, and I am. Hush." Every neuron in my brain tells me to stop. Not to do this because once I cross this line, I won't be able to stop. But I don't want to be logical. I want to feel.

She obeys, her fingers playing in my hair as I nip at her tender flesh through her panties. I'm too eager not to taste her soaked pussy. Too amped up not to go through with the exact thing I know I shouldn't. "Betty, do you understand what it means if I don't stop?"

Glancing up at her, she sinks her teeth into her bottom lip, her hips rotating as my finger lazily runs over her panties.

"Nothing changes," she breathes. "You still don't want me."

CHAPTER 13

BETTY

My body plunges into the icy depths of heartbreak as Nash pulls away from my center. Stretching to his full height, he gently lifts me off the dresser. The moment my feet hit the ground, I know whatever was about to happen is done.

I'd known better. I'd known it would mean nothing for him to kiss me, or taste me, but I wanted it anyway. Nash Donovan has lived inside me so long, infusing himself with my delicate tissues, that I was willing to take whatever crumb he was going to throw my way. Somehow, my heart overrode my logic, telling me it was better than nothing at all. It was something, and maybe that could be enough.

It wouldn't be, though, not once the moment passed, and he walked back out that door.

What the hell is wrong with me?

"I can't do this," he groans, running his hands through his hair and snatching his filthy shirt off the floor.

"You mean you won't," I correct him, choking back the tears that threaten to spill free. Tears he doesn't deserve.

"Yes. I won't because no matter what, I can't give you what you want." The volume of his tone rises, but he's not shouting at me. He's not angry, but clearly frustrated. Whether it's with himself or with me, I don't know, and frankly, I don't care.

How many times am I going to do this to myself?

How many times am I going to pray that Nash comes to his senses and he'll see we could be good together? That I could be everything he's ever wanted.

Stepping a fraction closer, my chin shoots high. "Maybe you should ask me what I want before you make assumptions." I shove past him, ready to open my door and let him out, but his hand grips mine, holding me in place.

"Betty, I'm not like that guy you went out with tonight. I'm not... settled. And despite what you've seen me like in front of everyone else, I'm not always like that. I can't give you a white picket fence in a neighborhood full of kids running down the street and Sunday dinners. I can't just stay here in Cole County." My arm twitches at my side, wanting to wrap him in a hug. He sounds almost broken. But why, when everything he's saying is wrong?

My mouth draws down into a deep frown as I stare at the man in front of me. So many times growing up, I thought Nash got me. It never occurred to me he didn't understand the burden of carrying my family name when he would inherit the family legacy. Maybe we did always see life differently. Shame on me for believing otherwise.

"If you took the time to ask me what I actually want, you would know you're wrong. Yes, I have had this undying crush on you my whole life. I have waited for you, pined for you, and gotten on my knees to pray for you, but I shouldn't have, and I won't anymore. You should go."

"Andromeda," he sighs as if pained by my words.

"Don't call me that. You don't get to call me that," I whisper. "At the very least, I thought we were friends, Nash. It's funny, through all of my pointless hoping and fantasies, I never expected it to happen. Then, you bought me those flowers and kissed me, and I actually thanked the galaxies that you were finally coming around. I thought this would be the best love story because we were friends first."

"I can't be your friend," he whispers, his head dropping to his chest.

"I know. For what it's worth, I'm sorry I put you in this position of temptation or whatever has happened between us twice now, but I'm done. My heart can't take any more."

Without another word, I exit my room, jog out the front door, and hop into my truck. I'm supposed to stay here if we have a full house, but I can't be around him right now.

I can't sit there and listen to his roundabout apologies and assumptions about what I want and need.

Ever since I was a little girl, all I wanted to do was leave Cole County. I wanted to leave behind the small town and travel the world so I could see the stars from everywhere. I wanted to know if they shone differently from place to place. For him to assume I wanted a perfect, cookie-cutter life here in Cole County is mind-blowing. I may have never outwardly said I wanted to leave, but my major should have made it clear enough. All the times I spoke about traveling with no roots should have been a giveaway.

My vision blurs as I speed down the road that will carry me away from Boulder Ranch. The road that will hopefully help me leave Nash in the rearview mirror, exactly where I should have left him a long time ago.

I've never been a big rodeo girl, but something about barrel racing has always drawn me in. Possibly because it's a female-dominated event. These women rip and roar around those oversized tin cans like it's nobody's business. They control the animals beneath them with poise and elegance that not everyone understands.

"Geez, she was fast!" I gasp, looking up at the clock as the current number three-ranked barrel racer gallops through the gate. Apparently, the competition was for the junior level, but several professionally ranked adults were also participating in a showcase—a simple way to keep the motivation high for the younger participants.

"Yeah, Tammy is something else." River snorts sarcastically.

"Is she still flirting with Gray?" Leaning heavily on the gate rung, I quickly eye River before the next rider comes charging out of the gate.

"Yes, and no. She's calmed down, but still always asks him to save her a dance at the Thirsty Pony." River runs her tongue over her teeth with a violent click.

"Seems like she's not the only one playing games then," I sigh, resting my chin on my forearm.

River only cocks a brow, staring at me. Worrying my bottom lip, I cave, knowing we're not leaving this spot until I explain myself. "So, Nash and I got into a fight last night after we almost... Well, that doesn't matter. He pretty much told me he's physically attracted to me, but that's all it'll ever be because he can't give me what I want. Mind you, his idea of what I want is completely wrong. I just want him."

"Um, didn't you have a date with Ward last night?" River links her arm through mine, cocking her head. We're not having this conversation out here.

"Yes," I groan, as we make our way back to the med room. "It was after. Um, I let Ward back in the house, you know, like for a nightcap maybe, I don't know. Then Nash showed up, and he was being such an asshole. I've never seen him like that before. Then we argued, and I left."

River draws out the word "Right," as if she, too, isn't convinced by any of this. Neither am I. How did this become my life? "So what are you going to do?"

"Try to stop torturing myself," I sigh.

River only nods as we tramp through the grass in silence before speaking up again. "Did you enjoy your time with Ward? Any sparks there?"

"Yes," I admit.

"Then see where that goes," River shrugs. "I don't appreciate Nash stringing you along, and quite frankly, I'm on the verge of letting Fester run him over for it."

A wet laugh leaves me. River is not always the warmest person, but she is there for the people who mean the world to her. I'm honored to call her my best friend.

"I'm terrified of Fester," I whine. "Please don't bring him around." River introduced me to her bull, and though he's been nothing but gentle, he's massive. I'm not tempting fate by letting that big boy out of the gate. "I think you're right. Even if it's not Ward, it's time I moved on from the past."

"Well, here's your chance," River grins, just as Ward jogs up to us.

He immediately pulls me into a hug, squeezing me tight. "I've been looking for you. Wanted to make sure you were alright after last night. Your brother seemed pretty worked up."

"Brother?" I nearly choke on the word. Of course Ward would assume that was my brother. I'd never named Beckett, only mentioned how close we were. "Um, Nash isn't... He's not my brother."

"Oh," he lets out a nervous chuckle, removing his cowboy hat to scratch the back of his head.

Placing a soft hand on his forearm, his eyes meet mine again. "Nash is an old family friend. Like a brother, I guess. I'm fine, though."

"I'm glad." Ward grabs hold of my hand, linking our fingers together. "Where are my manners? Hi, Dr. Thompson."

"Ward, you can call me River." My eyes gape, staring at the woman beside me. River doesn't extend that courtesy to very many men. She spent too many years of her career battling for the respect of the MD that follows her name.

I decide to take that as a good sign that she approves of Ward. Approval I don't need, but appreciate just the same.

"With all due respect, Dr. Thompson works just fine for now." He flashes her a sheepish grin before River nods my way and wanders off.

We watch her go as a soft breeze blows around us. Nervous butterflies soar through my stomach. I'm not sure what to say to Ward. I feel terribly about Nash's behavior, especially since I genuinely enjoyed my time with Ward on our date. He'd made me laugh and immediately opened up about his upbringing, goals, and childhood. It was refreshing not to have to extract information from a man.

"So what are you doing tonight?" he pulls my focus back to him.

Initially, I'd hoped to sit out by the lake and stare up at the stars, but with yet another storm rolling in, there will be nothing but clouds in the sky hiding them from view tonight. "No plans," I answer truthfully.

"Can I cook you dinner?" My insides melt. Ward is so sweet. Why can't I give myself to someone like him?

Newsflash, Betty. You can.

"You sure you want to spend two nights in a row with little old me?" I huff out a quick laugh.

He bends low, softly pressing his lips to mine. "There's nothing I want more than to spend my time with you."

CHAPTER 14

BETTY

I'd barely noticed the shift from spring to summer. How did April become July first? The heat and humidity are stifling. The air is so thick, it's like a wet blanket smothering you the moment you step outside.

Typically, this horrid weather makes me never want to leave the air conditioning of my home, but the past few months have been magical. Perhaps when we allow ourselves to be happy and live life to the fullest, the little things that typically stand out to us simply disappear.

Tugging at my thin linen top, the fabric already sticks to my skin. It's the week of the Summer Explosion in Cole County, so it's been an insane rush of tourists and preparations at the Miller house. Tate and I decided to add two cabins, which has taken more of my time than I had to spare overseeing construction during rodeo season. We hadn't expected so many to want to stay here, and it's proven to be a great stream of revenue for the ranch.

Fortunately, the competition night isn't until next weekend, but Gary and Rhonda Miller will be coming into town for the festivities that span the Fourth of July. What they don't know is we've planned a surprise dedication ceremony for them. They're wonderful people and deserve all the praise.

The extra responsibilities at the ranch have made it nearly impossible for me to keep up with multiple shifts at the bar. Jim finally hired some additional staff, so I've been able to spend fewer nights there, which meant more time with Ward. Speaking of which, he's the exact reason I'm late. The man insisted on showering together, which meant my hair got wet, and then I had to blow-dry and style it.

My brother is going to kill me. Once a week, we meet for lunch, and I've blown him off for the past few weeks because of my schedule. But there is nothing Beckett hates more than someone being late.

Sweeping my limp hair off my shoulder, I wave as I shuffle past the receptionist's desk in his office building. It's one of the newer miniature skyscrapers here in Carruthersville. A structure that speaks of the type of businesses that own or rent space here.

It's a mad dash through the hallways once I jump off the elevator, stopping at Beckett's office door to find a woman seated behind his desk.

Chocolate-brown eyes meet mine as she looks up from her paperwork. "Hi, can I help you?" Her voice is firm, but with a southern twang more pronounced than mine, confirming she's not from here. Honestly, she reminds me of River. No-nonsense with that shrewd stare and straight mouth.

"Um, this is my brother's office. Beckett Hughes?" I stay outside the doorway as if nervous to cross the threshold. There's no way I'm remembering wrong. I've been coming here for the past five years.

"Oh. Oh my goodness," she stands from her desk, straightening her cream pencil skirt. "You're Beatrice." She stops in front of me, extending her hand for me to shake. "It's so nice to meet you. Beckett talks about you all the time."

"Hi," I laugh nervously.

"Apologies, I'm Harper Brookes, the new estate lawyer here at the firm. I just moved to town. Beckett gave me his office and moved down the hall. I can show you."

"Thank you."

Beckett had mentioned that a new lawyer was joining the firm. He hadn't said anything more, and I hadn't asked. So much about his career flies straight over my head, so I don't even bother trying to comprehend it. He loves what he does, and that's good enough for me.

"Knock, knock," Harper cracks her knuckles against the doorframe.

The office is bigger than his previous one, with more filing cabinets and a massive bookshelf filled with law volumes along the wall. "Hey, Beck. Sorry, I'm late."

"No worries. Seems you met Harper here," he gestures, still scribbling across his legal pad.

"I did. Are you ready for lunch? I'm on a little bit of a time crunch." For good measure, I glance at my watch.

Without even meeting my stare, my brother hands me his card. "Better idea. I'm swamped with the ranch stuff. Take Harper to lunch, on me."

My heart sinks a little. It's been weeks since I had time alone with Beckett. I may have canceled on him over the last few weeks, but he has never canceled on me. Whatever he's working on must be super important. I guess I shouldn't be surprised since he, too, is now involved with Boulder Ranch as their tax lawyer.

Turning to face Harper, I give her my best Betty smile. "Well, looks like it's us then."

Together we move down the hallway, waiting for the elevator in silence. It's not until we step foot out on the sidewalk that she speaks again. "This weather is so much more stifling than in Alabama." Her long, delicate fingers fan her face as if that will provide any reprieve when the heat and humidity mix like this. It won't. You'll only sweat more.

It's a short walk to the cafe that Beckett and I usually go to. The small talk flows effortlessly before we enter the tiny restaurant. The conversation remains surface-level, but is comfortable.

Entering The Villa Cafe is like stepping into what I would assume an upscale coffee shop looks like in a big city. I've never been in one, so I can only make that assumption based on movies. The interior is alive with chatter, clinking silverware, and the lingering scent of Brazilian coffee. They say we've become caffeine addicts, and that couldn't be truer.

Harper leads us to a two-seater by the front window. Beckett and I always sit near the back as he's terrified someone will recognize him and interrupt our lunch, asking for legal advice.

"This place is so cute," Harper chirps.

"Yeah, we come here a lot." Glancing over the menu, I mentally slap myself. I already know what I'm going to get. It's the same every time. *Maybe that's your problem, Betty.*

For once, I study the menu harder. It's so hot outside, I can't imagine eating anything I would consider comfort food, yet my eyes pause on the meatloaf sandwich. I've never tried it, nor does it sound appealing, but it rattles my insides. Meatloaf is Nash's favorite.

"I've been eating nothing but takeout, so I should have a salad," Harper says absently, "But a loaded BLT sounds scrumptious."

I can only stare at her, absorbing her accent. Everyone has always told me how strong mine is, and I never really heard it until I listened to someone else. "Where did you say you're from again?"

"Oh, yes. The suburbs of Alabama. Grew up in a super uppity neighborhood, went to an Ivy League college, then to law school, married our family friend." My eyes go wide at her words. "Oh, no. Nothing crazy. He's only three years older than I am. Anyhow, we got married, I did all the things a southern belle wife from money should do," she sighs heavily as if recapping the past exhausts her. "Then we had my daughter Ainsley. She's eight. I wasn't happy, so I got divorced, and here I am in a new city where I don't know anyone and am trying to do things all on my own for the first time at the ripe old age of thirty-nine."

My jaw hangs loose, surprised this stranger just told me her entire life story as if it were nothing. But looking back, I shouldn't be surprised. It's always been that way. The Betty everyone has always known was always the person people could talk to. They could tell me their secrets, fears, hopes, and dreams, and know I would never judge, but listen and absorb every word.

"Wow," I breathe. "That's..." I try to find the words so I don't sound rude.

Harper waves me off with a nonchalant huff. "Yeah, it's fine. My daughter and I are happy with the move."

"What made you come to Carruthersville?" I ask as the server places water in front of us. We quickly give our orders, and then she focuses those big eyes back on me.

"It was the only law firm I got an offer from," she shrugs. "I applied to all sorts of places, but I was a lawyer who hadn't used their law degree in thirteen years. Fortunately, they took a chance on me."

"Well, welcome. I'd be happy to introduce you to some of my friends."

"Maybe. It's a little tough being a single mom now. There's no one but me to watch my little angel." A soft smile pulls at Harper's full lips, her sharp, layered bob swaying with the tilt of her head. She is by far one of the most stunning women I've seen. Tall, with high cheekbones and almond-shaped eyes.

"I understand, but if you ever need a break, I'm happy to help, and my mother has worked with kids her whole life. We always had tons of them running through the house, so she'd be happy to help too."

"You're a gem," Harper says, squeezing my hand.

Our conversation flows from there. Harper is an open book, telling me all about her family and her friends back home. It's like we've known each other for years, cackling over the craziest things as we devour our lunches, both of our plates clean in the end.

"My goodness, I'm so full," she leans back in her chair, wiping her mouth. "That sandwich was too large when I'm wearing a skirt this tight."

A laugh bursts out of me as I cover my mouth, before she sits up a little straighter, her eyes raking down someone behind me. I can feel their heat, and before I even turn around, I know who I'll find.

"Betty, we need to talk," Nash all but growls, pulling up a chair from a nearby table.

Harper's on her feet in seconds, her brows arched high as if assessing what type of mess I might be in. "No, please. Take mine. I need to get back to the office. Betty, I'll call you."

"Bye, Harper. See you this weekend."

Nash pulls out her seat and watches her leave before sitting down with me. "I tried calling you."

"For?" The word comes out clipped, but I have to protect myself against him. I don't want to sound snippy, but I'd been having fun. My little broken heart was finally mending with him, mostly keeping his distance. It became easier each day not to look back when I wasn't constantly seeing his handsome face or experiencing the way his voice vibrated through my chest and shot straight down to my core. I'm happy...

"Did I need a reason?" His tone is incredulous, and I want to slap him as much as I want to kiss him.

Dammit. His presence is undoing all the work I've done to move on.

"I have to go." Instead of waiting at the counter to pay, I slip some cash into the portfolio and turn to leave.

I've been successful at avoiding Nash unless it was in a group setting. He still stayed at the cabins every time he was in town, but with the system I implemented, there's no need for me to see him. I keep the main house booked with others, so he never has the chance to be that close to me, and it's worked. I've started to heal.

"Betty, don't walk away from me." Nash follows me outside. The clap of his boots only urging me to move faster.

Spinning to face him, he stops abruptly, our chests so close they brush with my deep inhale. "Why? We're not friends. According to you, we're not anything more than old acquaintances. We can continue to live our lives the way we used to and pretend nothing ever happened."

His jaw works as he stares me down on the sidewalk. "You know I don't want to be your friend, but I..." There goes that defeated tone again. The one that begs me to forgive him without speaking the words, but is unwilling to cave on his own.

I have no fight left. I'm so tired of this rollercoaster that is loving Nash Donovan. Why wouldn't he just let me go if he doesn't want me?

"Give me one good reason I should keep talking to you, Nash. You know this hurts, yet you keep coming back to gut-punch me again and again. Why?" My voice cracks. It's just cruel of him to keep doing this to me, and I'm an idiot if I allow it to keep happening.

He has the decency to flinch at my words, reaching for me only to drop his hand. "Because I'm not going to watch another man touch you."

And I don't know whether to scream or cry, so I do the only thing I can and walk away.

Rearview mirror, Betty. Rearview. Mirror.

CHAPTER 15

NASH

The only decent gym in Cole County is in Carruthersville, and I hate it. It's filled with all the types that I hate: the gym bros, the women who do nothing but cardio, the types that hog machines, chit-chatting while they catch up on life. But our county is full of small towns. No one has attempted to build a gym specifically for serious lifters or fitness enthusiasts.

I'd been on my way there when I stopped into the cafe for a chicken wrap and a shot of espresso. I'm exhausted from the constant travel and all the work I've been doing around Boulder.

It's work I chose to do for two reasons. One: I get to see Betty every day. Most days, she doesn't notice me, but I see her. She's fucking radiant with her summer tan and those long chestnut waves. I can't stop fucking looking at her or replaying the night we fought in my mind.

Two: I've known Tate and Gray since they were kids. Farming families stay close around here. They've had trouble hiring some extra help, so of course, I stepped in. I would do anything for those two. It aligned with my need to be here more anyhow.

The past two and a half months have been miserable. Ward seems to be there all the time. Apparently, he lives only a few counties over, so it's not hard for him to come to her. The worst are the nights they go back to her place, and I can't sit there and torture myself thinking about what they're doing in her room at the Miller house.

She's fucking everywhere. The ranch. In town. My head. Even at my parents' house, dropping off lasagna her mother made for them for their damn anniversary.

I'd come into town to get a workout in today. I need to release my frustration. Not only have I been watching Betty canoodle with that super nice guy who actually deserves her attention, but she's not the only reason I've been home more.

It was easy to pretend I just needed to spend more time with my parents. They'd told me they were healthy, minus the normal wear and tear of aging and ranch work. A little arthritis was nothing to write home about. I've already got a touch of it in my knees.

It turns out they lied. They didn't want to bother me. My mother was born with a weak heart. She'd had surgery as a child, but there was never a guarantee it would last her a life-time. Apparently, that lifetime is creeping toward the end.

At first, it only seemed like she didn't have the same stamina she always did out in the fields, then she noticed it became increasingly difficult to catch her breath. She tried to play it off as getting old and out of shape. An excuse I'd called her on. My mother could throw hay bales and carry calves by herself. She's put grown men to shame a time or two.

Spending every moment I could here was as much about my mother's health as my growing obsession with Betty Hughes.

My chest aches as I watch Betty walk away, but I refuse to chase her. Too many times I've messed with her emotions. I want her. I crave her skin against mine, but I still can't give her what she deserves.

This conversation isn't done. I saw the way her eyes lit up, staring into mine. She still wants me. She gets one more chance to tell me to fuck off. If she can convince me that's what she wants, then I'll be forced to leave her alone. Forced to watch Ward or someone else give her everything I'm too chicken shit to step up and do.

For now, I'm going to go clear my head with iron and sweat.

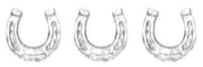

The influx of tourists this time of year makes my skin crawl. Cole County has become a popular destination for people from around the world, particularly for its holiday events. They all want to experience the charm of small-town living, as romance movies often depict it. And they have it right. No one does a celebration like we do, but thanks to them, traffic sucks, crowds swarm the bars, and the rodeo events are packed more than usual.

Attractions like horseback riding lessons and petting the cows and goats become an everyday thing at the ranch. Something the Millers always allowed because their home and ranch were open to everyone. They are so much like the Hugheses, with huge hearts and open arms.

It's been amazing seeing them again. Gary and Rhonda are just as warm and goofy as ever. Their new scenery has done nothing to change the people they've always been.

My phone vibrates in my pocket, drawing out my groan as I yank the device free. "What's up?"

"You almost here?" Gray grunts into the phone. "Need to get started tagging the cattle."

"Yeah, I just packed. Be there in a few."

"You're a lifesaver," he sighs as if I just lifted a weight off his shoulders. Gray works harder than most, managing Boulder alongside Tate and keeping up with his own ranch, River keeps adding animals to.

I only chuckle in response before ending the call. Gray and I weren't as close growing up, with him being the same age as Betty. The age difference was just enough to put us in different eras of life. It wasn't until he started riding here regularly that I made a more concerted effort to get to know the kid. He had it tough, but he didn't make it easier on himself. The number of times he picked a fight with his brother, Tate, when he could have just let it go, evens out with all the reasons he was justified in his frustration with their relationship.

It's a relief to see that they're good now. Running this place together and, from what I hear, even spending some quality time together. Family is important. Cherishing those relationships makes life worth living.

I snort to myself, knowing I don't make enough of an effort with my sisters. They have their lives, and I have mine. I try harder than they do, but not to the point of inconvenience. We call on holidays and birthdays, send cards, and they even text me pictures of my nieces and nephews. But that's where it ends.

A moment of enlightenment hits me as I saunter into the barn and catch Betty and Ward hugging as she laughs at whatever he says. I couldn't figure out why I was so adamant about not letting her go until now. Reflecting on family has me realizing that she has always been mine. And yes, that has changed now. She's not a little girl who's just a nerd obsessed with stars. She's a grown woman, and this is more than physical attraction. It's irrelevant if I want it to be.

Family doesn't always mean blood. It's the people who accept you for who you are and who want to be in your life despite the flaws. They're the ones who choose to be by your side even when you don't deserve their support. They give you their hearts even when you stomp on them because they love you.

Maybe I'm too late to claim Betty as mine, but I'm not done trying.

I watch her and Ward from the entryway for long, agonizing minutes before he pecks her mouth and disappears toward the back. Marching forward, my dominant side takes over. She wouldn't talk to me yesterday, but she's damn sure going to talk to me now. Snatching her hand, I drag her behind me, ignoring her protests.

Leading us in the opposite direction Ward practically skipped off to, I suck in several deep breaths in an attempt to calm myself down. The moment we clear the corner, I spin her around, allowing her back to crash into the barn wall. She releases a tiny yelp, and my cock twitches, hoping she'll make that sound when I sink inside her for the first time.

Releasing her wrist, I put a foot of space between us. The longer her skin touches mine, the more likely I am to pull the same shit I have the last two times I kissed her. Then her wide eyes meet mine, and I can't stand to be so far away from her. *Fuck!* Dropping my palms to the wall beside her head, I cage her in. Betty overwhelms my senses with the pump of her chest and the way her lips part before her tongue runs over them.

"I am going to ask you this question one time. You are going to be completely honest with me."

Her warm breath fans over my face before she once again licks her lips, averting her gaze. Ever so slowly, she rotates her head back to center, and our eyes lock. Heat blazes in her stare, revealing everything to me without her words. The way she feels about me is alive in her soft brown eyes.

"Nash, you have to stop," she pleads.

"Answer my question first." She remains silent, pressing her back against the wall as if she can put more space between us. I only lean in closer, just enough so we're no more than an inch apart. "Do you still have feelings for me? Any at all?"

"Please don't make me answer that," she whimpers. Such a pretty sound from those full lips.

"Answer it, Beatrice," I demand, though I do my best to keep my voice soft. The caveman shit only ever comes out in the bedroom. But Betty brings this side out of me. Every part of me wants to claim her, but I tried to stay away. I tried to tell myself all the reasons this was a bad idea. The first being that she's a sweet girl. She wants a sweet man like Ward. Right?

I'd convinced myself of that, but we kept getting drawn to each other, and she kept reminding me I didn't know what she really wanted. So I spent some time thinking about it and concluded that I don't care what else she wants. I'll give it to her as long as she wants me too.

"Yes, Nash. You have lived in my heart and my head since I was a kid. I can't shake you, and damn, I've been trying. I have been trying to move on from you for real this time. Ward…" She swallows loudly before continuing, "I found a man who's good to me and I like him, but he's not you. They never are, and that kills me because you've never truly given me the time of day, not even when I told you the truth. So, yes. I still have feelings for you, and I probably always will. Are you happy now?"

I lean in closer, wanting to kiss her so badly. I needed to hear her say the words. My muscles literally shake as I fight to restrain myself. My face hovers over hers, our lips almost brushing as I speak. "Then you can't be with him."

Shoving off the wall, I turn and walk away. It's a dick move, but Gray still needs me, and I need to cool off before I fuck this up again.

CHAPTER 16

BETTY

My heart hammers in my chest. What just happened?

With Nash, I don't know whether to go left or right, up or down. He reels me in and casts me out to sea again when he sees fit, and my stupid heart falls for it every time.

I can't catch my breath as I lean against the barn wall, my hand clutched to my chest.

"Betty?" Ward's voice startles me, my feet leaping a solid foot off the ground as he comes into view. Irreversible sadness lives in his eyes, his jaw muscles flexing under the stubble as he draws closer to me. Tugging his cowboy hat off his head, he comes to a stop in front of me, rolling his lips before he speaks again. "Are you in love with him?"

"What?" I breathe, my eyes darting side to side as if that will hide my obvious reaction. "With who?" An unnecessary question when I know he means Nash.

His booted feet bring him closer, the scent of hay and dirt wafting up my nostrils. A smell I've grown used to spending so much time here at the ranch. It's become a comfort. I'd thought it was because of Ward, but now I'm not so sure. "Betty, I really like you. I do." His fingers wrap around mine. "But if you don't want this... if you want him... I'll accept it."

"There's nothing going on between Nash and me." My words release as a whine. A tenor that even I would usually wince at. "I promise you." My fingers squeeze his, hoping my words are convincing enough, even though my heart is shouting what a liar I am.

I do really like Ward, too. We've had so much fun together, and he's helped me separate myself from Nash, at least on a surface level.

There's nothing between Nash and me but a few stolen moments and decades of my life pining after a man who decides when and how he wants me. I didn't quite lie about that.

"I heard everything." He releases my hand, taking a step away. Devastation draws at his features, his eyes turning glassy as if he actually might cry.

"Ward, I swear." I step toward him, but he once again moves out of my reach.

"Betty, I wanna believe you. I wanna just go back twenty minutes to when we were so happy, and we were kissing like a pair of teenagers, but..."

"Ward, please." I've never begged a man to want me. Not even Nash and I loathe that I am now. But part of me believes he might be the only way that I can let go of my childhood crush.

"You need to decide who and what you want. I won't be with someone who doesn't want me the way I want them. Once you know who you want, let me know." Dejection coats his words as he turns on his heel, drops his hat on his head, and walks away.

For the second time in so many minutes, I'm stuck here, wondering what the hell just happened?

Nash gave me an ultimatum.

Then Ward broke up with me.

Can I even call it that when we never made anything official? Do people still call it that in their thirties?

Shaking my head, I suck in a ragged breath before pushing off the wall. With every step away from the barn, my emotions war between heartbreak—again—and anger. Not just with Nash for starting this whole mess, but myself for not being able to tell him to get lost, and Ward for not believing I want to be with him.

That wasn't what he asked you, Betty, I chide myself as I stomp back to the Miller house. I need a shower, some tea, and maybe a few shots of bourbon.

The bustle of daily ranch life booms around me, but I don't hear it. I hear nothing but Nash and Ward's words repeating one after another.

"Then you can't be with him."

"You need to decide who and what you want."

Over and over again, their demands run through my mind. Nash has been the only man I have truly wanted my entire life, but Ward helped me see how much more I deserve than what I've had in the past, including my ex, whom I thought would be forever.

Punching the code into the front door, a blast of cool air hits me. It's enough to break me out of my trance. There's work to do before I meet up with River and her childhood friend Sadie tonight.

Grabbing water from the fridge, I check my messages.

River.

Tate.

My mother.

Beckett.

Jim.

Nash.

"Why can't you just let me go?" I groan, stomping through the house, tossing my phone on my bed, and then disappearing into the bathroom.

A shower will help. It will solve everything.

The groan of the pipes as I turn the shower nozzle makes me wince. It's so damn loud, but I guess that's to be expected in an older home like this. Although it has been updated over the years, the foundation dates back to the early 1800s. Those bones are still there.

Testing the temperature, satisfied that it's hot enough to burn off the confusion of the day, I strip out of my clothes, leaving them in a pile on the floor. Usually, the mess would make me cringe, but today I don't care.

Running my hands through my hair, I let the water soak into the strands. A smile crests my lips, remembering all the times Ward has done the same motion. His strong fingers combing my hair back so he could kiss me sweetly. The images flash and then disappear before I pile shampoo into my hands.

My scalp prickles as I massage the lavender-scented soap into my hair, the suds multiplying before they smack onto the tile floor. It takes longer than it should to rinse every drop of shampoo free before lathering the length in the matching conditioner. Securing my hair in a clip atop my head, a new image flashes before my eyes.

My palms curl around my neck, sliding over my clavicles, only to grab hold of my heavy breasts. My core tightens in response, the muscles clenching, begging for hands. His hands. Nash's rough palms roam over my skin, consuming me. Those skilled fingers pinching my hardened nipples painfully as he whispers against my throat.

You're mine, Beatrice.

"Yes," I moan, allowing my hands to drift lower, grazing over the top of my pelvis. "I've only ever wanted to be yours."

Then, as if someone snapped their fingers, the image fades. Gazing down at my hand, my fingers tremble, the tip of my middle digit seconds from rubbing along my sensitive clit.

"Dammit, Betty. Get it together."

Lathering my sponge, I quickly wash my body, determined to leave the fantasies behind. Allowing my eyes to drift shut, yet another finds me. Ward's lean frame presses against my back, his palms lightly gripping my biceps, while Nash presses against my front. Nash's lips trail over my throat as his hard length presses against my stomach. But it's Ward's fingers in my hair while he kisses the spot behind my ear that makes me moan.

They both whisper their demands.

Pick me.

I'm the one you've always wanted.

He can't give you what you need.

No one knows you like I do.

It's a back-and-forth ping-pong match as their hands and mouths trail over my skin. Their voices begin to blend until I shout, "Leave me alone."

My eyes pop open, and it's just me in the shower. My hand holds a crumpled sponge, and all the soap is gone.

It seems I can't even trust myself.

Cutting the water, I grab hold of my robe, shrugging it on though I haven't dried my skin at all. Water drips from my body as I exit the standing shower, stopping in front of the Jack and Jill sink. Steam covers the expanse of the massive mirror, my hand swiping across the glass so I can see my reflection.

Empty, unfocused mocha brown eyes stare back at me. It's the same woman I've always known in my reflection. The one who worries about everyone else before herself and longs for things so far out of reach it's laughable to believe they could ever be mine.

When you grow up resigned to a fate that was chosen generations before you, those things live as fantasies in your mind. They give you something to wish for, though you already know those types of wishes don't come true.

Toweling my hair, I head toward my bedroom, ready for a fresh set of clothes. A reset.

My door creaks as I grab hold of the knob, entering my room. With one more shake of the towel through my hair, I flip my head back only to gasp so loudly I want to cover my ears. "Nash..."

CHAPTER 17

NASH

I'd expected Betty to run into my arms at the sight of me.

She claims she's always wanted me, but now I'm unsure as I watch her features shift—shock to heartbreak to unbridled anger. Not even a split second passes as each emotion flashes in her eyes.

Standing from the bed, each step is slow and deliberate as I move toward her. The type of approach used with an animal to avoid startling them with sudden movements.

"Andromeda, what's wrong?"

She only stares at me, her eyes never leaving my face as I take two quick steps, closing the distance between us. But nothing changes in her expression. Fury burns, and her soft mouth twists into a nasty grimace. That gorgeous face is transforming into one I've never seen. One I don't recognize.

"Andromeda," I try again.

"What's wrong?" She drones as if she's not even there. She hasn't moved an inch when my fingertips finally graze her cheek. "You want to know what's wrong?"

"Yes," I cup her chin. I'd overheard one of the guys saying Ward looked like someone had run over his puppy. Not that I wanted the guy to get hurt, but I assumed Betty ended things with him. That's the only reason I'm here. It seemed like she was choosing me.

"You," she whispers, before her eyes meet mine. "Nash, you're what's wrong. You're hot and cold nonsense put me in a terrible position."

"I'm sorry." But she holds up a hand, stepping out of my hold.

"I was moving on from you. I was finally starting to believe I could exist in a world that didn't revolve around Nash Donovan." Her words are washed in anguish I hadn't expected her to feel.

Reaching for her again, her eyes only narrow on me. Her quick steps put her out of my reach. Only my words might bring her back to me now. "You've never had to," I insist.

A gut-wrenching sob escapes her. A sound that nearly brings me to my knees. Even if I hadn't given in to this new-found obsession with her, that sound would have ruined me. I've known Betty too long, and her brother would hate me for hurting her like this.

"Yah know, Ward heard us. He broke up with me," she sniffles, roughly swiping her hand beneath her nose.

"Andromeda."

"Stop calling me that," she squawks. "Just. Stop." She sounds defeated, and part of me wants to do everything I can to erase that feeling. Another part of me knows I should just walk away. "You had the chance to want me, and you didn't until you saw me moving on. I was happy, Nash."

"Look, I know I've been hot and cold. I've been telling myself all the reasons not to pursue you, though you left me an open door repeatedly. But I..."

"You what? Wanted to act like every other man? You didn't want me before, so why now?" she shouts.

Words fail me as I stand there staring at her. I should be able to tell her all the reasons. She's gorgeous and smart, but really the only good excuse I can give her is jealousy. I'd been fine allowing her to maintain her crush while I kept my distance until I saw another man's hands on her.

"That's what I thought," she sniffles, before shifting to the side and gesturing toward her door.

Without another word, I leave her room. She's right. I'm just a divorced guy who lives on the go, and I've got almost a decade on her. Head bowed, I exit the house and hop into my truck.

There are two choices: I can either take her as mine or I can do exactly what I should have done from the beginning.

Keep my distance. Keep our relationship platonic as it's always been. But I know I can't do that. I've tasted her. I've touched her. That sweet pussy was seconds from pulsing around my tongue.

Yanking my phone out of my pocket as I fly down the road, I dial Hunt. "Don't you have cows to wrestle or something?" he groans into the phone, his voice deep as if he'd been asleep.

"Funny. What do we have pending?" I grit my teeth, gripping the steering wheel so tightly that my knuckles turn white.

"Nothing has changed since yesterday. You're supposed to be taking some time with your family," he sighs. There's a rustling sound in the background, as if he's climbing out of bed. This man loves himself an afternoon nap, so he can burn the midnight oil and still get to the gym at five a.m. every day. "That was our deal, Nash. I handle the business, and you spend time with your mom, unwinding a bit. You've been so tense since last summer."

My teeth grind again. Yeah, I have, and it has nothing to do with the fact that my mother's heart is failing, or I'm now responsible for keeping my father's business running; it's Betty Hughes. The woman has me in knots, constantly battling myself and everything I've ever told myself I need and want.

"Let me know if anything changes," I grunt, ready to hang up the phone.

"You know it's okay to be happy, right? The divorce fucked you up, whether you've ever admitted it. You can want something different from the life you had here with Katherine."

"Get out of my head."

"Not a chance," he chuckles. "Give me a call after your mom's appointment next week."

Angling my truck toward my parents' ranch, I decide to take my friend's advice.

It takes twenty minutes to reach my family home. Pulling up the drive, I spot my mother in her rocking chair on the porch, sipping lemonade she likely made from scratch this morning.

Her smile spreads wide as I hop out of the truck and make my way to her. Mine spreads too. There's no stronger woman than my mother, both physically and mentally.

Raking my gaze over her face, her age is finally starting to show. She hadn't looked so drawn the last time I was here. Her skin still seemed vibrant, and there was energy in her movements. Now I see the struggle. I can see the fight it takes her to push out of her chair and how her hand grips the railing tighter with each step down the front porch stairs.

"Stay there, Momma, I'm coming to you," I scold her.

"Nash, you stop it. I'm perfectly fine. The exercise is good for me." Her words are sure, but the labor of each word pushes through. She can't hide from me, and I can't hide from the fact that she's getting sicker.

We meet at the bottom step, her hand slipping into mine. Does she feel even more frail today, or is it my imagination? I've always had a creative mind. That's why consulting has worked well for me. I'm able to construct deals from nothing that turn the sale into everything for both sides.

"Come on, Momma, let's get you back to your chair." She snorts in annoyance, but leans on me as we trek the same six steps she just fought to come down. A heavy breath leaves her as she settles into her stark white rocking chair. Her chest rises and falls with increased exaggeration several times before she once again sips her drink out of a clear glass. "Can I get you anything?" I ask.

"No, baby." She pats my hand lightly, smiling fondly at our land that stretches far enough you can't see the main road from here. "Aren't you supposed to be at the ranch? Gray says you've been out there every day."

"When did you speak to Gray?"

My mother waves me off, her hand shaking slightly as she brings her glass to her lips before it clanks back onto the arm of the chair. "You know your father has clunky joints. He's been seeing Gray's wife, Dr. Thompson, over in Harper's Hallow now. He happened to be leaving while we were coming a few days ago."

I'd almost forgotten Gray had married a doctor. None of us could have ever seen that coming. He'd become a broody

asshole to most, but that's also because he was usually inter-
acting with Tate. At least his brother felt something for him.
My sisters probably wouldn't even notice if I disappeared.

"Everything okay with him?" It hurts to swallow, like there's
a boulder lodged in my throat, waiting for her answer. Guilt
settles in my stomach, knowing that I've stayed away long
enough I've missed my parents' aging. I forgot that they might
have needed me.

"Nothing a few injections and some pills can't fix for now,"
she grins.

"Like pain medication?" I sit up a little straighter. Pop always insisted he wouldn't take the stuff, not even when he
broke his arm and needed surgery, or when he had an impacted
tooth removed when I was ten. He didn't touch any of the pain
medication he was given.

"They're not getting me addicted to those chemicals," he'd
said. We tried to convince him he was wrong, but my dad is
as headstrong as they come. He suffered through the pain and
didn't complain once.

"No. No. Um, I think they're called in-saids." Her mouth
screws to the side as if she'd had trouble saying the word.

"Ah, so just anti-inflammatories," I sit back in my seat,
breathing normally again. There's only so much upheaval I can
handle at once right now.

"Yes! Yes, those." My mom grins widely, slapping my thigh in triumph. "They're helping him."

"How are you, Momma?" Her tired blue eyes meet mine. Where my father has the dark blue of the deepest ocean, my mother's are as pale as they come. Eyes that should be icy and could appear cold have only ever exuded warmth.

"Baby, I'm gonna be fine. It's just a rough patch, but you know what you could do for me?" A glint sparkles as a mischievous grin spreads.

"Anything for you, Momma."

"Bring me a grandbaby before I die," she winks.

If only she knew that's one of my top five thoughts about Betty Hughes. That woman pregnant with our baby is what I dream about most.

CHAPTER 18

BETTY

My flyaways stick to my forehead and neck as I exit my car in the small lot down the street from the bar we're meeting at for girls' night. River insisted Gray would pick me up, but I needed those few minutes alone. I've avoided nights like this since college, when I no longer needed to pretend I actually enjoyed them. Not to mention the confrontation with Nash has me twisted in knots so tight I'm not sure I'll be able to undo them.

Sweat coats my palms as my nerves kick in. This was to be a small thing, but the list kept growing. River invited Sadie and Joy. Joy is bringing her friend Reyna. Then I invited Harper. I figured that if we were adding to the list, we must all need this night off.

I wasn't sure Harper would say yes, but then the woman practically jumped at the opportunity to get out of the house. Her parents are in town for the Summer Explosion festivities, and so she had a built-in babysitter.

There's a lazy vibe as I enter through the front double doors. With low lighting, the red interior is set ablaze, creating a mysterious ambiance. Massive leather couches surround tables with low-lit candles, both lining the walls and positioned at the center of the space.

River had mentioned the grand opening about a month ago, and we thought it would be a great place to try this weekend. Tourists crowd the smaller towns, but they tend to avoid larger cities such as Carruthersville and Harper's Hallow. They're too much like what they can get at home.

Plus, tomorrow is the big parade, and they have the beach meetup after. I hadn't joined them last year, but River assured me it was a massive reunion. Fun time or not, I won't be there. You can find me on my couch with a movie playing, avoiding the crowds.

"Betty!" Joy calls, waving me toward a massive curved corner booth. All the girls are here, including a stunning woman I don't recognize, but Harper is still missing. Checking my phone, there's a text from her.

> **Harper:** *Running 20 min late. Be there soon.*

> **Me:** *No worries. I just got here.*

"Hey," we all smile as I hug Joy, River, and Sadie. "Betty," I introduce myself to Joy's friend Reyna.

"Betty, this is another one of our childhood friends, Amalie. She's a new mom of twins and definitely needed a night out," River introduces me to the glamorous woman beside her.

"Hi," I smile wide, shaking her hand. "Is your husband with the babies?" I ask, taking the drink River shoves at me.

I notice that she and Joy are the only ones with soda water. I say nothing, though. It's possible that River is exhausted from the workday, and who knows about Joy? Alcohol puts me to sleep as if I were hit with a dart tranquilizer when I'm that tired.

"Yeah," Amalie rolls her eyes. "The big baby was scared to be with them alone for the first time, so he's got his sister and my mom there with him."

We all laugh. Men can be such babies, but that's to be expected.

Time seems to pass at a rapid pace as we sip our drinks and gab about nothing. It's nice having women I actually enjoy spending time with. There are several girls from high school I still see from time to time or keep in touch with, but mostly our lives don't align, and that's okay. But for once, I don't have to pretend to be happy, or bubbly, or fun. I can groan and roll my eyes or be disagreeable, and the world isn't crumbling at my feet.

I've had my brother and the bar, and now I have Miller Inn and River and...

Well, there's no Ward anymore, is there? If I go to him and tell him I choose him, my eyes will lie. My heart will eventually betray me because it still belongs to Nash. And that will only hurt him more in the long run. I refuse to do that to someone else.

I'd considered what Nash said to me today. Every word has been turned over in my mind a million times. I shouldn't believe him. His actions have only shown that he is here to do nothing but play games. He has proven time and time again that he can't honestly want me or care because otherwise he wouldn't string me along, knowing how I feel about him. No good person would do that.

So, I then considered that maybe Nash isn't the good man I always thought he was. Maybe he's nothing more than this image I concocted in my head at ten years old. I've seen other sides of him these past months. Angry. Possessive. Sweet. Aloof. Uninterested. You name it, it's been there.

But I felt him too. I felt his response to me and the way he held my cheek and kissed me. The question isn't whether he finds me attractive. I think that much is clear. He does. His body reacts to my touch, and his eyes smolder with heat. But being attracted to me isn't what I want from him.

I want it all. I want everything.

"Hey, sorry I'm late," Harper's southern chirp pulls me out of my thoughts as her hand finds my shoulder.

I stand to hug her as we slide over to make room for her on the end. "Ladies, this is Harper Brookes. She's new to town and working with Beckett at the law firm."

They each wave, introducing themselves one by one.

"Tell us about yourself," Sadie says, flagging the server for another drink. She, too, is a new mom. For a minute, it makes me wonder if something is in the water. I'm fairly certain I heard Joy is pregnant, too.

Staring down at my drink, my stomach churns. Perhaps if there is something in the water, it will affect my ice, too.

My hand runs over my soft, flat stomach, remembering that time in my life. A time when I thought I'd found someone I could spend forever with, though I was in love with another man. Ryan and I had been happily dating for three years. Our relationship progressed as it should have, culminating in our decision to move in together after two years. Everything was fine. We were fine, and then everything changed.

In an instant, my world seemed to fall apart. *We* fell apart. It wasn't because of him but because of me. I never told him the truth. Only my mother knows what happened.

I retreated into myself and pulled away until we called it quits. That's when I moved into my apartment. That's when

I rebuilt myself, but one thing remained... the stars in my eyes when I thought of Nash Donovan.

"Mommies unite," Amalie cheers with her drink in the air. "We have babies, but that just means you can help guide us. We're both first-time moms," she points to her and Sadie.

"At least Rhodes did the single-dad thing for eleven years first. Gives us a head start." Sadie takes a long drag through her straw.

I'd swear she was still pregnant the way her skin glows and those mismatched eyes of hers sparkle.

"Single parenthood is no joke," Harper concedes, crossing her long legs.

"What happened to the father, if you don't mind my asking?" Amalie chimes in.

"We got a divorce. I wasn't happy, so I left. Pretty simple. He still wants to be part of her life, but he's in Alabama, and we're here." Harper shrugs as if it's no big deal. I've never met a woman so unbothered by everything, and it's refreshing as can be.

"Well, there are plenty of cowboys to choose from," River snorts. "Just ask Joy and me. We picked the grumpiest ones." They laugh in unison as if they share some magical secret. I suspect they do. Those two snagged the Garrison brothers. Plenty of women had their eyes on those bachelors, but they never gave them the time of day.

"I'll keep that in mind," Harper snorts, sipping her drink again.

Our group laughter rings through the bar, but we swiftly change the topic to stories of the past. Their antics from the beach party last July's Summer Explosion and warnings for Harper about Old Man Wilber and his dog Patches, our favorite two menaces in Cole County.

"He's ridiculous. It wasn't enough that I came here to help when he broke his femur. Oh, no..." Sadie waves her hand through the air, her long ponytail swaying with her movement. "This man decided he is once again going to climb the same tree because he's not paying someone to do something he can do on his own, and..." she pauses dramatically, a single finger held in the air, "He still plans on riding next week." Sadie's hand slaps her bare thigh as if in disbelief that her grandfather is so crazy.

She's not. She knows, but she worries about him. It's sweet.

"Rides what?" Harper breathes.

"Bulls!" Joy, River, and Sadie all groan at once.

"Is it bad that I might want to see that?" Harper chuckles, just before River's gaze tracks somewhere behind me. Her eyes immediately light up, only for Joy, Reyna, and Sadie's to follow.

Spinning in my seat, a line of men approaches us. The Garrison brothers, Rhodes with a baby carrier strapped to his front—how he got in with that is beyond me—and a man I don't recognize, whom I assume is Reyna's man.

"Ladies, let's go," Gray mumbles.

We're all on our feet in seconds, hugging and promising to do this again soon. The ladies fawn over Rhodes, bouncing him and Sadie's son, making cooing noises while we finish up. I keep my back to the moment as my stomach churns once more.

Linking my arm through Harper's, we head out behind the crew when a male voice stops me in my tracks.

I swear the universe is doing everything in its power to keep this man in my path, and it feels like torture.

Harper leans in close, whispering in my ear. "Isn't that the same guy from the cafe?"

"Yeah, I am," Nash stops in front of us. "Do you need a ride home?" he asks Harper.

"No, I'll manage." She hugs me again before exiting the bar with the rest of our group, leaving me alone with the man I can't seem to escape.

I move to follow them, but Nash links his fingers through mine, keeping time with me. We step out into the heat of the night. Dallas, Amalie's husband, is parked at the curb, the two of them leaning in the back, checking on the twins.

So many babies... I'm distracted, fighting the nausea that makes bile creep up my throat when Nash's words pull me out of it. "Can I take you somewhere?"

"Why?" My brow scrunches in confusion.

He tucks a piece of hair behind my ear, running his thumb over my cheek. "Because I have to prove to you I meant what I said."

Dammit, if my heart didn't just skip a beat.

CHAPTER 19

BETTY

My palms sweat as I stare up into Nash's blue eyes. I know I should say no. I should walk away because this only ends one way. This ends with me in tears and heartbroken all over again.

How many times will I let the same cycle repeat itself?

Yet, there's an emotion I've never seen before alive in those swirls of blue. They seem to open like the depths of the ocean, allowing me to peer into the depths of his soul. It's unnerving, but draws me in.

Nash has been in my life since I was a kid. He's steady, quiet most times, but has always been kind. He has always been respectful and would go out of his way to help another person. That's the version I'm in love with—the man I knew growing up. Sure, I'm aware of the life he started in Montana. He found love once, the way I thought I had. It's the surface-level parts of him I know in the present, but with the way he's looking at me now, it's as if I can see all the nitty-gritty pieces that linger beneath. The things he reserves for the people he loves most.

It's that look that leaves my fingers trembling as I place my hand in his waiting palm.

The moment our skin touches, his smile lights up the night. The one he used to wear as we laughed around the table for Sunday night dinners. Every tooth is on display as the corners of his eyes crinkle.

"Where's your truck?" He pointedly checks up and down the sidewalk as if it will miraculously appear.

"The lot down there." His eyes track where I point before linking our fingers and leading the way.

We don't say a word. Still, the silence between us is comfortable. I wonder what he's thinking. Is he as nervous as I am about whatever we're going to do? His focus seems to shift between the street on his left and somewhere past me on the right.

The liquor warms my belly, contributing to the electrical sparks with every brush of Nash's thumb over my knuckles. It provides comfort I easily melt into, as if he only wants to remind me he's here. We're connected.

"Keys?"

Digging in my purse, I hear them jingle but can't seem to find them amongst all the crap I carry around with me.

"One sec," I huff out a breath.

"Baby, you need to have your keys out before you get to your truck. You'll be safer that way." I want to roll my eyes at his overprotective nonsense. I've worked in a bar for years, and I can handle myself. Cole County isn't some crime-ridden place where it's not safe for a woman to be out at night alone.

Releasing his hand, I keep digging, only to pause. "Did you call me, baby?" My gaze shifts up to meet his, that grin once again stretching wide.

"I did. Problem?"

It's as if my brain short-circuits. Heat creeps up my cheeks, and I have no idea how to respond to the pet name. Andromeda is one thing. That dates back to my childhood, but baby. That's... My heart flutters in my chest as butterflies swarm my belly. It's finally happening. Nash is for real this time.

"Um..." I'm still searching for words when my finger finally slips through the key ring, the solar system chain attached to it making Nash laugh.

"You still have this?"

"Of course," I snap, offended he's laughing about it. "Beckett gave that to me for my twelfth birthday."

His fingers tuck that same chunk of loose hair behind my ear, grazing my cheek. I melt into his touch. This is all I've ever wanted: his kindness, his touch, his heart. "I remember. I was there. It was a Sunday dinner, and you insisted on keeping it on the table, flashing it no less than fifty times."

"You remember that?" I breathe, semi-stunned that he would recall such a meaningless event for himself as he ushers me into my passenger seat. Warm breath fans over my face as Nash leans in close, his mouth hovering over mine. The scent of his cologne wafts up my nostrils as his eyes shift down to my mouth and back up to meet my stare. Just a fraction of an inch, and his mouth would be on mine.

Every breath is labored as I wait and wait and wait. "Betty, it may have taken me a minute to notice the woman in front of me, but you were my family growing up. Nothing means more to me than family. Never forget that."

A harsh swallow is forced down my throat as he leans his head to the side. My tongue darts out, wetting my lips, ready for him to consume me and set my insides on fire once again, but he only pulls away, tapping the side of the truck. "Seatbelt," he nods before shutting the door and stalking around to the driver's side.

"Goodness gracious," I release a ragged breath, my hand resting on my chest.

The energy between us is more charged than it's ever been. And I don't know how to handle it.

Once again silent, Nash puts the truck in reverse before pulling out of the lot and swinging us onto the road. The AC is blasting the way I'd left it, but I roll my window down, leaning out, allowing the warm night air to wash over my face.

"Are you cold?" he asks.

"No." I allow my eyes to drift shut and just exist in the moment. The fresh air and the sounds of a bustling small-town-county around me, full of cheer, and pops of fireworks in the distance. Cole County is home. It always has been, but when I close my eyes like this, I can pretend I'm somewhere else. The same set of stars shines bright in the sky, but the land is different; the seasons and people have changed. In my mind, I can be anywhere else but here. "I'm a windows-down all year-round kind of girl," I respond softly, as a lazy smile pulls at my lips.

The soft whir of the driver's window descending pulls my focus back to Nash's side of the truck. He, too, has his window down now, his arm resting on the edge more relaxed than I've ever seen him. The veins along his forearm pop while his thick hair blows in the breeze as we fly down the open road.

I hadn't realized we were moving toward the outskirts of town. The areas where there's still open land, and the ranches and farms are all you'll find.

Angling my body toward him, I bend my leg up enough that my heel can rest on the seat and my chin on my knee as I grin his way. "Where are we going?"

"You'll see."

"Fine. Then tell me about your life." Regardless of whether Nash breaks my heart again, I want to know him—his likes, dislikes, what brings him joy, and his greatest fear. I want to see the world through his eyes.

He chuckles softly, placing a hand on my thigh, rubbing absently along the bare skin before responding. "We're almost there."

I barely hear his words as his touch sears my skin. I'd forgotten I was wearing a dress when I cocked my leg up on the seat. From his angle, he'd be able to see my bright pink underwear.

My mind and body battle. One telling me to have some modesty and drop my leg, the other telling me to spread them wider. If he wants to look, let him. It's what we want too.

It's then that I notice his eyes keep darting to the apex of my thighs. Moisture already pools there. It had been from the moment he took my hand in his. He'll see the wet spot if there's enough light, but I don't care. I need his eyes on me. I need him not to stop things tonight.

Gravel crunches as he pulls onto what must be a private drive. There's nothing but trees and land. Not a thing until we're about half a mile down the road and the dense trees part to reveal a small cabin.

"Where are we?" I ask, contorting my body to stare out of the front windshield as he parks my truck.

He doesn't answer, climbing out to open my door. I take his hand, hopping out too. My eyes rake over the quaint space.

It likely only has a single bedroom, judging from the exterior. The wood has worn over time, but the structure seems solid.

Once again linking his fingers through mine, Nash leads us to the front door, unlocking it and then allowing me to step inside.

The interior is modern yet cozy, draped in hues of hunter green, brown, and taupe. It's clean as if regularly inhabited, and the scent of pine fills the space—the same pine as Nash's cologne.

Nash moves behind me, his hands cupping my biceps as he dips his mouth close to my ear. "Welcome to my home."

CHAPTER 20

NASH

There was a plan: give Betty space.

It was simple. She'd been furious and hurt, understandably so. I pride myself on being a man who doesn't screw with women's feelings. Anyone I've slept with since Katherine has known exactly what they were getting. No matter how many times we fucked, that was all it was ever going to be. I wasn't looking for a new wife. I wasn't looking for anything. There was too much on my plate with work, and I had no stability in my schedule. How could I foster a genuine relationship when I could be gone for a day or three weeks?

It's why I had put aside the notion that kids were an option for me a long time ago, too. It never happened with Katherine. With our divorce went that dream. I was okay with that. I was content with my life until Beatrice Lola Hughes barged back into my life like a fucking bulldozer and professed her undying love for me in a drunken stupor.

Had she said the words sober, I would have laughed them off as the fun-loving woman pulling a fast one on me. She was always the life of the party in her younger years. Beckett kept me up to date on all things Hughes-related, and these are small towns. Everyone knows everyone. There are no secrets in places like this.

If she hadn't been so drunk she could barely stand, I would have been able to brush it off as nothing. I wouldn't have looked at her as a woman for the first time. I wouldn't have ogled her body and wondered what her naked flesh felt like under my palms. My mind wouldn't have even entertained the thought that we love her laugh and the way she scrunches her nose when someone irritates her, but she still forces her best Betty smile.

None of this would have happened had that night gone differently. Nash wouldn't be so eager to know the woman and her quirks and what makes her smile, so those stunning brown eyes sparkle. He wouldn't need to be around her every second of every day or allow anyone else to see his possessive side when someone else didn't hesitate to be with the amazing woman she is.

I was going to give her space. I was going to let her choose when she wanted to have an honest conversation with me. When we stood there in her bedroom and she asked me why, the only answer I had was jealousy. It wasn't good enough, and

I wasn't going to potentially miss out on a chance to make this right with her with some lame-ass words.

After leaving my parents' house, I came right back to the ranch. As I stalked back out to the stables, tacked up a horse, and then rode out to the outskirts of the Boulder property line, I had time to think. As creepy as it sounds, a part of me has always adored Betty's company. When she was younger, it was in a brotherly or friend-type way.

Just the same, I enjoyed listening to how she viewed the world. She sees the world in these vibrant colors. Many of us miss them because we're so caught up in our own lives that we never take a minute to appreciate them.

I haven't had time to learn much about how her life has turned out as an adult. I was around less, and she worked as much as I did. Our encounters were random more often than not until she took over the Miller house, and I took over for my dad. It's as if those pivotal moments in our lives brought us back together, and all I've done is fuck it up over and over again. Yet, she keeps giving me chances. We're drawn to each other no matter how much I tried to talk myself out of it.

"Home?" she questions.

"Uh, yeah. I've owned this cabin since I graduated from college. It's where I stay when I'm in town." My palms lightly squeeze her biceps again before she turns to face me, my arms immediately looping around her waist.

Her arms remain limp at her sides, her chest arched back as if trying to put space between us. Space I don't want.

"No. You always stay at the cabins on the ranch. Even when there's nothing going on." Her dark brows scrunch low as if searching for another explanation, only to meet my gaze again, her mouth moving awkwardly.

My heart thumps in my chest, hoping she can see everything I'm not saying written on my face. I stayed at the Miller house because she was there. It was the only way I could see her all the time, even when I was constantly pushing her away. It's how I slept at night, knowing I was close to her, though we weren't curled up in the same bed.

It's funny, I thought her feelings for me were absurd. Betty spent twenty-three years of her life being obsessed with me. How? Then, in less than a week, the same happened to me, and I haven't been able to put her out of my mind either.

I didn't want to go there because I was sure I wasn't what she wanted. Not really. Her childhood dreams were skewed and wrong because she didn't know the man I'd become. Still, witnessing her moving on with someone else broke something inside me. I no longer cared what I thought she deserved as long as she still wanted me. I'd become that man if it meant I could hold her and listen to her laugh every day.

"Because of you," I whisper.

"Nash," she melts into my hold, her chin dropping to her chest.

Not allowing her to protest, I grab hold of her hand and lead her out back. The poles for the hammock had been in place when I bought the property, but there was no net. It seemed symbolic at the time, as if I was jumping on my own for the first time, and I was. Unlike my classmates, I didn't get a job straight after graduation. I took the money I'd saved over the years, bought this place, and started building my consulting business.

Sitting in the new hammock I'd added a few years ago first, I carefully drag her down with me. She giggles, protesting before swinging her legs in, smoothing her dress, and lying next to me in a stiff plank. I leave my arm behind her head, stroking her shoulder as we stare up at a dark but cloudy sky. I'd hoped the stars would be out for her tonight, but I'm just glad she came here with me.

"You wanted to know about my life. It's pretty simple, but here goes." Clearing my throat, she shifts to her side so she can watch my face. I want so badly to kiss her, but those moments have gotten us nowhere so far. "After college, I stayed in Montana. I'd been dating Katherine for a few years at that point. She became my person, my home away from home. We were friends who worked well in a relationship. I've never told anyone but her and my best friend, Hunt, this, but I loved being away from Cole County. I knew I'd have to come back at some point because Pop would eventually turn over the distribution business to me, but until then, I wanted to live a life outside of small-town USA, so I stayed, built my company, married Katherine, and kept a low profile. Then I would come back here and see my family, and I realized home wasn't always a place. It was the people. I missed my people."

A long breath fills my lungs as I go silent for a moment. Yet Betty keeps her eyes on me, patiently waiting for me to continue. The heat of the night turns our skin sweaty, but I don't care. Something about this moment seems so cathartic for us. For me.

"Anyway, Katherine and I were married for ten years. We worked non-stop on our respective companies and built that massive house that has never been a home. I liked it in Montana, so it didn't matter. She wanted it, and I wanted the land to have my own ranch, but I never found the time to build it. We never had a family, and over time, we realized we should never have gotten married. It was okay that we were always meant to be friends, and so we got a divorce. I stayed, and she left." Betty tenses beside me, but I don't ask her why, assuming it's just in response to my deadpan sob story.

As if reading an encyclopedia, I'd recounted the high points of my life. They aren't necessarily the important things now, but a base I wanted her to know so she could understand me better in time.

"Did you want that?" she whispers.

"What?" I ask, pressing a kiss to the tip of her nose. There was no helping it. My lips needed the feel of her skin.

"A family."

"Yes, but that doesn't matter now." She only nods, allowing me to continue. "So here I am, forty, going on forty-one. All I have is my consulting, my friends, and the distribution business. My life is pretty boring, but then you woke me up, so thank you."

She nuzzles in closer, wrapping an arm across my middle. "My pleasure."

CHAPTER 21

BETTY

As children, there were no limitations to our dreams. We believed in magic, dragons, and ghosts. Over time, the pressures of becoming adults and contributing members of society snuff out those dreams. As we become workers, mothers, and fathers, we are often forced into roles that may not have been our first choice.

But here in this hammock, under the night sky, with Nash talking to me about his life and nothing at all, I can suspend every belief. His thumb never stops rubbing my bare shoulder, comforting me in a way I can't express with words. It's the most I've ever heard him talk. He's always been able to hold a conversation or speak on a topic when needed, but just as often, he could sit in complete silence.

Thunder rumbles in the sky, the temperature dropping just enough to send a chill over my warm skin. "You cold?" he asks.

"A little," I yawn, arching my back so my breasts press into his side.

A groan escapes him, his hips shifting as if trying to adjust himself. It would do me no good to let my gaze move down his body, so I focus on his face. "Come on, Andromeda. Bedtime."

There's humor in his tone. Watching him fling himself out of the hammock, almost falling to his knees before he stands and reaches for me, I can't help but giggle. I had imagined romantic, lazy nights like this with Nash my entire life. In many ways, the reality is even more amazing.

The moment we're back inside, his hand finds my waist, holding our bodies flush. "Thank you for bringing me here. It was nice getting to know adult Nash." My hands find his shoulders before my fingers sink into the soft hair at the nape of his neck. "I should get going," I whisper, my gaze flicking to his lips before meeting his eyes again.

That same charge passes between us. His warm breath fanning over my face as if he's struggling to exhale properly. His moan stretches and vibrates through his chest as I run my fingers through his hair, lightly scraping my nails over his scalp. I somehow never noticed how much taller Nash is than I am. Maybe because we've never had a chance like this to just stay in the moment, holding one another as if we're both terrified to let go.

"It's late. You can stay," he whispers against my lips. "Just to sleep."

My mouth is dry as I try to respond. My lips part, but nothing comes out. Our bodies only press closer together, Nash's mouth slow to lower to mine. Where my body had burned with endless flames the two other times we tasted one another, it's a low simmer tonight.

Our mouths slant, exploring each other for the first time. The passion remains between us, driving the temperature to a feverish high, but there's no frenzy. No need to rush through the moment as his fingers dig into my hips and hair. "Stay," he breathes against my mouth when he finally pulls away.

Butterflies soar through my belly. This is what I've always wanted. He's right here, and he's not running. He's pulling me in; he's trying.

The past reminds me I may regret this. He might back off again, but life is about taking chances. I took one to manage Miller Inn, and I can take one more on Nash. What's the worst that could happen?

Pressing up on my toes, I place one more soft kiss on his lips. "I need pajamas."

A growl rumbles through his chest as he grins down at me. Weaving his fingers through mine, he kisses my knuckles before leading me to a room off to the right. That cheesy grin never leaves his face as he digs through a drawer, pulling out a shirt and handing it to me. "I can grab you pants too if you want, but I doubt they'll stay up."

"Shirt's fine," I give a tight-lipped smile, raising it.

"Bathroom is through there," he points behind me. "There's a smaller bedroom across the hall with a pullout. I'll be in there if you need anything."

"You asked me to stay, but you're going to sleep in another room?" Disappointment coats my words. I wish it didn't. I wish I could be Cool Betty from back in the day, where nothing fazed me. But everything about Nash sends my world topsy-turvy, and I don't know what to do about it.

He's in front of me in seconds, running that same thumb along my cheek, before tilting my chin up so our eyes meet. "Do you want me to sleep in here with you?"

I nod, not trusting myself to speak without sounding like a squeaky mouse. The corner of his mouth quirks before he softly caresses my lips with his. His touch is gentle and searching. My lips part, waiting for more, needing more. Breathlessness seems to hold me in place, waiting for Nash to make a move. Always waiting.

"Go change, Betty." Turning me away, he walks me to the bathroom door and then closes it.

Clutching the shirt to my chest, I just listen. The dresser opens again, then closes. Then there's the rustle of clothes over skin before they're tossed aside. Then the soft slap of his bare feet across the hardwood floors as he leaves the room.

My shoulders drop knowing he still chose to sleep across the hall. Stripping out of my dress and bra, I splash water on my face and knot my hair in a messy bun on top of my head. It doesn't matter what I look like. Nash won't see me anyway.

Slipping on the shirt, I inhale its scent. It smells just like him—the woods and crisp fall air. The hem hits just above mid-thigh. I'm not a tall woman at five-four, but I'm all legs. With a deep breath, I exit the bathroom only to jump back into the doorframe as Nash stands in the center of the room with two glasses of water in his hands.

"Shit, you scared me," I pant, clutching my clothing to my chest. "I thought you, um, left."

My nerves are firing, being in Nash's bedroom with him, wearing his shirt while he wears nothing but some low-slung gray pajama pants that leave nothing to the imagination. My gaze rakes down his chiseled abs, to the deep V at his hips, before I force my eyes to meet his again.

Don't look, Betty. Don't mess this up.

"I get thirsty in the middle of the night," he says, raising the glasses. "And you've been drinking, so you're gonna need this." There go those butterflies, fluttering around in my belly at the kind gesture. "Get in the bed, Betty."

My body is primed to obey his every demand, so I fold my dress, tucking my bra between the fabric before placing the items on the corner of the nightstand. "Which side?" I whisper, staring at the massive bed as if it would matter. Both of us could lie starfish in the bed and barely touch.

"Betty," the bass in his voice lowers as he takes a sip from his glass. "Get. In. The. Bed."

My swallow is loud as I shuffle to the closest side, sit, and then swing my legs up onto the mattress. Nash places a glass on the nightstand beside me and then slips into the bed on the opposite side.

The click of the lamp turning off bathes us in darkness. My hands stay folded over my chest, my muscles taut. Even my breaths seem not to want to release as if terrified to spook him out of the room. Nash remains perfectly still for several minutes before he drapes his arm over my middle and tugs me into his body. "Hey," I yelp as he chuckles.

"You wanted me to stay. I want to hold you."

I let him wrap me in his arms, pulling me into the heat of his bare chest. My heart somersaults, cheering on the moment.

Close your eyes, Betty. You're finally getting everything you want.

CHAPTER 22

NASH

It's been a week since I brought Betty to my cabin. A week since we started this journey together.

We've kept it between us, stealing moments and sharing kisses every chance we got. Neither of us has taken it further than some heavy groping. It makes me feel like we're teenagers again, but I want her to know I'm serious about this. I heard her, and I thought this through. I want her.

The rodeo crowd seems louder than ever, as if they know what the Garrisons planned for tonight. It's a night to honor Gary and Rhonda Miller. It was the Miller family who started this ranch generations ago, and until Tate bought it, it had always been in their family. Though if you ask them, it still is. The Garrison brothers made Boulder Ranch their home, and they will continue carrying on the legacy. A legacy I am honored to be part of.

Placing my cowboy hat on my head, I step out onto the track bordering the arena. I told Betty I would continue to stay in the cabins so as not to draw attention to us, but I want nothing more than for people to know she's the woman on my arm. Yet, she hasn't pushed for us to be out in the open.

There's no room for me to blame her. I've come and gone so many times that the woman might have whiplash. I can understand her wanting to be sure I will hold to my word and not push her away at the first sign of my discomfort.

I hope she's seen my effort this past week. Despite our kisses being little more than stolen moments most days, we've talked every spare minute. Sometimes during walks around the land or by the lake. Other times, on the phone or if I can sneak into her room at the ranch without being seen. Learning everything about that woman might be the single best thing I've done in a long time.

"Hey, Nash!" I spin to the sound of my name, Old Man Wilber gimping his way toward me.

"Hey, Wilber. Great to see you." I pull the guy into a hug, his hand clapping my back harder than necessary.

"You too, son. I hear you got your nastiest bulls out here tonight," Wilber grins like the fool he is, showcasing a glint of mischief in his eyes. It seems as if he has been around forever. The guy does everything someone his age shouldn't, and his damn dog is always getting into something, yet I don't see the mutt at his heels.

Flashing him a quick grin, I nod. "Those men are here to compete. Might as well compete with the best."

The old man grunts, nodding absently as he waves at someone behind me. He's always been a celebrity in our fair county. If you don't know the Crawleys, you definitely don't belong here. "Save the nastiest one for me."

"Wilber, you are not riding tonight?" My words are a groan. I'd been warned he'd wanted to put on a show this weekend, but I figured it would be some ridiculous speech.

"Damn straight. I entered to compete like everyone else." His thick brow furrows as if challenging me to tell him otherwise.

I can only shake my head with a huffing laugh. He does what he wants to do. He's never cared about what anyone thought of him. It was that piece of his personality that helped propel me forward in my younger years. Take chances. Go for what you want. Enjoy life while you're at it.

Somewhere along the way, I forgot that last part. I've worked myself to the bone at my company, at the gym, and on my family's ranch. The past week with Betty has been the most I've laughed in a long time. The most I've relaxed and not counted the minutes or worried about the schedule. It was me, her, and whatever was ahead.

"Why you look like you're daydreamin' or something?" Wilber grunts, his weathered eyes crinkling heavily as they narrow my way. "You got yourself a new lady finally?"

"Finally?" I cock my head back, surprised he knew I was married in the first place. I rarely brought Katherine here. She didn't want to drive, and I preferred not to fly if I was going to be here for longer than a few days. There was a difference in travel styles, but it was never a point of contention. Looking back, much of our lives were like that, but our friendship stayed solid. It's probably also why our marriage was really never anything other than friends having sex and a guaranteed date to weddings.

"It's been what?" He cups his chin as if in deep thought. "Six years?"

"Uh, almost eight."

Wilber claps me on the shoulder in that fatherly way he always has. "Well then, time to hop back in the saddle, although it looks like you already have. Just stay away from those young things. You ain't no spring chicken no more."

"I'll keep that in mind," I groan.

I'm ready for this awkward encounter to continue when a group of calf ropers turns the corner, each greeting Wilber like the king of Cole County he is. Ward catches my stare, his glare a reminder that any chance we had at a friendship disappeared when I claimed Betty for myself. I don't even care.

She should have been mine from the beginning. Really, I should thank him for keeping her off the market for me.

What the hell, Nash? Who thinks like that?

Betty brings out my possessive side to the nth degree. She makes me jealous and obsessive. There's nothing I crave more than her eyes on me, her laugh, and her taste.

"Nash." Ward shakes my hand, ever the gentleman.

"Hey, Ward. You ready for tonight?"

"I'm always ready," he nods before falling back into conversation with the group.

I take that as my cue to slip away. I need to do one more check of the roughstock before the ceremony begins. It was something my father taught me from the beginning. *"Never trust someone else to do what you should do yourself,"* he'd told me time and time again.

Shouldering my way through the crowd, I can't control the grin that pulls at the corners of my mouth. Just five hours and then I'll have her back in my arms.

Stalking my way to the barn where the bulls and calves are held, I'm lost in my thoughts of her. She'll stay here tonight while all the rooms are being rented out, but hopefully I'll be able to convince her to come back to the cabin once they all check out.

It was our one and only night together. There are these prickling devil thoughts in the back of my mind that I hadn't even deserved that. That it might have been my one chance to have her. That dominant monster within that comes out in the bedroom growls in my chest, pissed we haven't gotten to sink into her core yet. We haven't felt her walls flutter around us or heard her moan our name as she comes all over my cock.

Yet the gentleman my father raised me as praises me for doing this right. For respecting her and just allowing myself to revel in the feel of her in my arms. Reminding myself that if I do this right, there will be plenty of time for it all, even if there are a million reasons I should let someone give her a better life.

Running through my roster of competitors for the weekend, my phone suddenly buzzes in my pocket.

It's rare anyone reaches out on rodeo nights. The close circle of people I keep in my life knows I'm focused. When I'm in work mode, I'm not one to be disturbed.

My brow scrunches low seeing my lawyer's name on the caller ID. "Hello?" I answer, confused by the call at six on a Saturday evening. I'm sure the man works day and night, but I'm likely one of his easier clients.

"Hi, Nash. Sorry to bother you, but we have a huge problem."

"With what?" My heart rate skyrockets, wondering which deal has gone so far off the rails that my lawyer needs to get involved. It's happened a few times throughout the years. Usually, some long-lost family member or offspring crawls out of the woodwork claiming rights to the land or property. My guy hasn't lost a battle yet, but that's because I'm pretty sure he's a mob lawyer. From the slicked-back hair and the custom suits and thousand-dollar shoes, he walks, talks, and fights like criminals are his highest clientele, and he's determined to make you believe they're not.

"It's the Kaufman deal."

"What about it?"

"You're going to want to get back to Montana. Now."

Fuck.

CHAPTER 23

BETTY

Nash: *I can't meet up tonight.*

Nash: *I'm sorry. I'll call you later.*

My heart sinks. Nash and I were supposed to get together after the rodeo to walk along the beach. He'd said he hadn't done it in years, and it was likely where we'd be free from the crowd and prying eyes.

It's only been a week since we became... well, I don't know what we are, but it feels like we're moving in the right direction.

No, it felt like we were moving in the right direction until he just texted saying he couldn't see me tonight. There wasn't even enough time for me to respond to his first text before the second one came in, effectively cutting off any attempt to question why.

So here I am sitting on the edge of my bed, alone, trying to pretend like I'm not upset. Like, I'm not worried he's pulling away from me all over again.

Was it something I did? Something I said?

Is he already bored with me?

Tears burn behind my eyes, and I hate myself for crying, especially when I don't know what's going on. He mentioned his mom isn't doing well. Maybe it was an emergency with her, or an animal was injured. It's happened before. Last season, River practically operated on a bull before Gray showed up.

It could be nothing. *It's fine, Betty.*

It's a fight to go through the motions before bed. My limbs seem to be filled with cement as dread weighs me down. The minutes stretch as I stand in the shower, my head tilted against the wall. I'm too scared to move, because I might collapse on the floor and no one would find me.

When I finally do move, I don't even bother drying my body or hair, simply slipping into my robe and then under the covers of my bed. I lay there hugging my pillow, staring at the ceiling. My mind won't quiet. It keeps replaying every moment I have ever interacted with Nash over the years.

Every second plays through my mind. From the night he found me in the grass staring up at the stars to the night of his last football game, when my dad and Beckett held him up on their shoulders, and he'd hugged me because he loved the hand-drawn sign I'd made for him. Then to every Sunday night dinner, and a few days ago, when he took me out in the fields with one of his horses.

He'd been so surprised I'd never ridden one, so he helped me up before hopping into the saddle behind me. His firm hands guided my movement as he coached me on how to use the reins and my legs to direct Casper. Turns out that was his favorite movie growing up, so when he got his first horse, a stunning white beauty, he named her after the friendly ghost.

Before I know it, the morning sun peeks through the curtains. Still, I don't move. I don't feel like I can.

I didn't hear from Nash again. Not a call or a text. Nothing.

Part of me wants to call him and demand he tell me why he blew me off this time, but I also don't want to lose whatever we found. So I lay here, clutching that same pillow, telling myself I hadn't made a mistake giving him a chance instead of trying to repair things with Ward.

It will all be fine.

If only I believed it.

I can barely keep my eyes open as I slug into my parents' house, ready for our weekly Sunday dinner.

Nash was supposed to be here.

He'd asked if it was okay, which I thought was so sweet. Neither of us thought that his showing up would look suspicious. Still, I wanted to hold off on telling Beckett anything was going on. He understood. *"When we tell our families about us, I want you to be sure you're mine,"* he'd whispered against my lips.

I already was. I always have been. But it meant so much that he respected my fears. He understood I was waiting for the other shoe to drop, and it seems as though that was with good reason, though he assured me he would prove himself to me.

My eyes press shut as I fall into the kitchen doorframe, the thud forcing my mother's gaze up to me.

"Betty, sweetheart, are you okay? Are you ill?" The back of her hand immediately presses to my forehead. I didn't think I looked that terrible. Then again, I barely managed to slip into sweatpants, a ratty off-the-shoulder t-shirt, and a bra. There was no tugging the brush through my knotted hair, so it sits in a lopsided bun at the top of my head.

"I didn't get any sleep last night." I try to wave her off, but she insists on pressing her hand to both cheeks, my forehead again, and then to my lymph nodes. "Mom, I said I'm fine. I'm just tired."

"Don't you snap at me, Beatrice Hughes."

My head bows, chin pressing to my chest. I'm not one to dive into the extremes of my emotions, but it seems that's all I've done since that first kiss with Nash. "I'm sorry, Momma. Can I help with anything?"

"Just go sit down. You look like death. I'll make you some tea."

A weak smile tugs at one corner of my mouth before I shuffle to the living room, checking my phone for the millionth time. Still, there's nothing from Nash. The morsel of hope I was clinging to fades away as I stare off into space.

Noises filter in and out of my consciousness in the background, but there's no focus. There's no real comprehension as I wallow while berating myself for falling for his charming smile and warm hugs.

I knew better.

And I still dove headfirst. The worst part is knowing I would do it all over again. When it comes to Nash Donovan, I'm putty. I'm weak.

"Betty!" Beckett waves his hand in front of my face. "What's wrong with you? Are you sick?"

"Can you all stop asking me if I'm sick?" I grumble, shoving up off the couch. "I'm tired. Running the inn is a lot of work."

Beckett holds his hands up, backing away, and I instantly feel horrible for snapping at him, too. It's not their fault that my heart is in shambles at my feet all over again because I've gone less than twenty-four hours without hearing from my...

"I'm sorry, big brother." I hug him around the waist, giving him three squeezes the way I always did as a kid.

He holds me back, resting his chin on my head. "If it's too much..."

"It's not. It was just a busy weekend with the Miller's ceremony and the rodeo. I'm okay, I promise." It's a lie, but I hope he believes it because I can't fathom telling my family the real reason I look like a zombie's cousin.

"Betty, I know you're tough and will work your ass off. It's probably the only thing we have in common. You can't keep running yourself into the ground, though. Have you talked to Jim about quitting the bar altogether?" There's so much concern in his eyes. So much love. I want to tell him everything. Beckett and I have always been close. He's always been someone I could confess my worries to, and he'd give me his advice and then hold me afterward.

Many never understood how we could be so close when we're five years apart, but it's the Hughes way. We support each other. Family is everything and always comes first, no matter what.

"I'm slowly phasing out of the bar," I say as we move toward the dining room. "I rarely work more than once a week these days."

"Good," he hums, kissing the top of my head. "You're too smart to be a bartender."

I know he means nothing by the comment, but it stings.

Astronomy has always been my passion. It's the only field I ever wanted to work in, but there's no place for it here in Cole County, unless I wanted to teach, and that is definitely not for me. Even then, it's not a solo subject. It wouldn't be my sole focus.

I might be smart, but not smart enough to avoid falling into Nash's trap again.

It's only another ten minutes before we sit at the table to eat. My mouth waters as my stomach growls loud enough that my father's stare snaps up to me. I haven't eaten since yesterday afternoon. It wasn't on purpose. I'd spent most of the rodeo in the stands with Harper and her daughter as we watched the kid consume popcorn, cotton candy, a massive soft pretzel, and two hot dogs. She could put grown men to shame.

But I was also watching for glimpses of Nash. He caught my eye once, grinning widely before tipping his hat to me. We seemed fine. What changed?

I busy myself, keeping the small talk light, as the conversation revolves around the Millers and the competitors from last night. It's almost enough for me to forget about my aching heart until my father brings up the source of the pain.

"I thought Nash was coming tonight." My father stabs another piece of pork chop before popping it into his mouth. "Did you see him before you left?" he asks me.

My mouth goes dry, my heart hammering in my chest, wondering if they suspect that there's something between Nash and me.

"Oh, shoot. I forgot to tell y'all. He went back to Montana," Beckett interjects before shoveling a forkful of mac and cheese in his mouth.

And my heart sinks. "Excuse me."

CHAPTER 24

BETTY

"What's the plan again?" River grunts as we attempt to hold my tiny suitcase closed, the contents spilling over the edges as if we're going to be gone for more than four nights.

An exaggerated sigh leaves me, my head falling back in frustration. "I'm gonna ask him what his problem is." Slumping onto the bed, I cover my face with my hands, not wanting to see the look on River's face. "You don't understand. We were so good for a week, and then after the rodeo, he just disappeared back to Montana. Then I found out from my brother that Nash was back in town, and they went out drinking together. I've gotten exactly five text messages from him in the past week and a half and not a single call."

"I'm not the mushy type, so give me some grace here, but we've talked about this. You decided before it was time to let it go. Then you chose him over Ward. But, Betty, when someone shows you their true colors, believe them." River rubs my leg with pity shining in her soft green eyes.

She's right. He's shown me he doesn't care. "I just need closure, but I also really am curious about the whole breeding selection process." It's the truth. Since starting at Boulder Ranch, I've immersed myself in the ranch and rodeo world as much as I could. My mind is one that needs to understand my surroundings. The ins and outs, as well as the nuances, are all important, so I don't let anyone else down.

River wrinkles her nose. "I really thought you just said that because you wanted to come. Gray made me watch a 'breeding' video, and I could have done without it." She gags before we devolve into a fit of laughter.

That's how it always is with us. No matter how serious the conversation, there will be good food and laughter. They say your friends can also be your soulmates. If that's true, River is mine.

"Okay," she pats my thigh. "I need to pee again, and then we're out of here."

I only chuckle as I try to zip my suitcase. It's the second time she's had to pee in the forty minutes she's been here. It is the dead of summer, though, so we're all chugging fluids like a fish out of water.

"Ladies!" Gray barges through my apartment door. I don't even know how he got in. The door should have been locked, and the lobby requires a fob.

"Coming," I grunt as I drag the zipper the last inch, breathing heavy.

I'm sprawled on the bed panting when I hear River giggling and the noises of the two kissing floating in from my living room. My body jerks forward as my gag reflex kicks in. How can I want to gag, cry, and cheer all at once? I'm happy for my best friend, but I miss Nash too. That had been us when we snuck moments alone together.

Get over it. It was a week, I groan to myself, shoving off the bed.

Rolling my tiny suitcase down the hall and into the living room, Gray doesn't even pretend like he wasn't seconds from stripping his wife and screwing her on my living room floor. Can I even fault them? They're like love-sick teenagers, but they are exactly what the other needed.

Gray always says I'm the one who brought out River's fun side, but he did that; I only amplified what he teased out of her.

"Is this what it's going to be like all weekend?" My mouth scrunches to one side.

"Last I checked, you were the one tagging along," Gray drops an arm over River's shoulder, kissing her temple. "Breeding is not in your job description," he chuckles.

Chewing the inside of my lip, I wonder if River told him the other real reason I wanted to come. My life forever revolves around Nash. Maybe this weekend will be the end of that.

"Fine. Let's go." I shake my head, rolling my suitcase past the pair.

Gray immediately takes it from my hand, lifting it by the handle and stalking through the door. It's weird watching another man carry my luggage. You hear about chivalrous men who do that kind of thing all the time, but other than Nash and my brother, I can't even remember a single man I dated holding the door for me.

My best friend definitely got a good one.

Every joint seems to pop as I stretch awake in the backseat of River's SUV. We drove the first fifteen hours yesterday before stopping at a hotel.

It was a typical chain you can find anywhere. There was nothing special about it. The rooms were nice and clean, and I had the space to myself, but I couldn't sleep.

It was an endless night of tossing and turning. I couldn't find a comfortable position, and when sleep finally took me, I would bolt awake. My dreams had fooled me into believing that my comforter shifting or my head rolling on the pillow meant Nash was climbing into bed with me. I'd wake, but he wasn't there. Then the tears would come, and I'd repeat the cycle all over again.

Pressing back into the seat, I attempt to stretch my legs as far as they'll allow. I couldn't be more thankful we took her car instead of Gray's truck, though he's been trying to talk her into a pickup truck if she's going to keep buying animals to bring home to their ranch. River only argues that her SUV trunk is plenty big and safer for transport. Any of the larger animals would require a trailer, and she's not driving a truck with one of those anyhow.

I'm not sure how long I was asleep or where we are, but the mountain landscape is stunning. Staring out my window, the possibilities seem boundless. A hopeful grin attempts to pull at the corners of my mouth as I imagine what the stars must look like dotting the sky above the mountaintops.

It must be breathtaking.

The scenery quickly changes, taking us through a small town with a mix of quaint shops and chain stores. A reminder of Carruthersville and the home I've always known. A pang of homesickness hits me, only to drown me in the acceptance that Cole County is the only home I will ever know.

"Morning, sleepyhead," Gray chuckles from the driver's seat. His eyes meet mine in the rearview mirror, but I don't match his smile. I don't feel like it. Not today.

"You're too chipper right now," I grumble.

"Well, I had an entire car ride worth of the soundtrack of your snoring. Why wouldn't I be?"

My mouth falls open as River swats his arm. "Don't be an ass."

"I like your ass," he snickers, squeezing her thigh.

I only groan. My snoring is why I never had sleepovers as a kid. I've always sounded like a frickin' dump truck, and popular Betty couldn't let people know she made noises that matched a foghorn.

My heart suddenly seizes in my chest. Nash hadn't said a thing. Is he so deep a sleeper that he never heard me or... *Stop it, Betty*.

You'd think, as a woman in my thirties, the stupid shit I obsess over when it comes to Nash would be nothing. That I wouldn't care or think about silly details like my snoring or if I said the wrong thing. You'd think I wouldn't care. That whole "take me as I am" mindset should be firmly in place by now, but I'm living proof that a woman can still hold on to those insecurities because no man has ever made her feel safe enough to let them go.

"Ignore him," River throws her husband a look of pure annoyance. "He snores louder than you do. Especially if he's been riding. I had to buy earplugs."

"You did not?" Gray gasps, tearing his gaze away from the road to glance at her, just as we turn up a steep drive.

"I did. Watch the road."

He doesn't say another word, returning his hand to her leg as we ascend the endless dirt drive.

A massive black modern home comes into view. The type that would belong to a billionaire determined to live off the grid, not a rancher from Cole County. How many people live here with Nash?

Ducking to peer through the windshield, my features scrunch as I attempt to take in all the sharp angles and overlapping wood paneling against the matte black. "Wow," I breathe.

There's no denying that the house is breathtaking. By no means would I ever have thought Nash would live in a place like this, and it's not my style, but it belongs in a magazine.

Gray only harrumphs as if confused by what he's seeing. "Doesn't seem very Nash to me."

"Didn't he build it with his ex-wife?" River asks absent-mindedly.

It's as if I can't breathe through the pain stabbing me in the gut. It's never been a secret that Nash had a wife. I never met her, but she was part of his life for thirteen years. She shared a life with him I had always dreamed of, in this house that he had built for her.

I'm lost in my head as I slide out of the car and toward the front door. River's at my side, her voice muffled in my ears.

This was a mistake. I shouldn't have come here.

I'm seconds from turning around, calling a cab, and high-tailing it to the closest airport. It's not too late to turn around and go home. A notion that dies the moment the front door swings open and Nash comes into view.

Nash stands there in dark-wash jeans, a fitted white T-shirt, and bare feet. He looks just as amazing as ever. Rested and as happy as he's always been.

Then his eyes meet mine, and I know I made a mistake. He doesn't want me here.

Chapter 25

Nash

I t takes everything in me to steel my features. Every muscle flexes, forcing me to stand there and look unfazed at the sight of Betty. She's here on my property, waltzing up to my front door, arm in arm with River.

Her shoulders roll forward as a sure sign of defeat, averting her gaze from my face. I haven't seen her since the rodeo. My life seemed to fall apart overnight, and I needed to handle it all. I had to shove her to the back of my mind, or I would have said, fuck it, and handled none of it.

I haven't been accountable to someone in over eight years, and even before then, in my marriage, I wasn't accountable to Katherine. I told her I had something to handle, and she waved me off with a smile. There was no explaining myself or checking in. Betty isn't the same, though. It's written in her eyes how much the distance has hurt her.

I did not intend for my actions to hurt her, and when Gray said they were bringing her, I finally had to sit down with myself. At first, I tried to lie to myself. We've been texting over the past few weeks. Then, scrolling through my text messages, there were only five from me and a dozen from her, most of which I didn't even answer.

So I tried to lie to myself some more. Someone surely told her I was out of town on business and that my mother's failing heart landed her in the hospital. It was no one's responsibility but mine to be honest with her. I'd asked that woman to choose me, and then I disappeared. I'd hate me too. In fact, I do. Betty is the last person I would ever want to hurt.

"Come in," I gesture to her and River, while Gray juggles their luggage. Shaking my head, I jog down the four steps, taking the smallest suitcase from him. I remember her stashing it in the corner of her room at the Miller house.

"Thanks," Gray grunts, hiking his duffel over his shoulder, then rolling what must be River's suitcase.

"Glad you guys made it," I clap him on the back in a half-hug as he steps into the entryway, dropping the bag. My insides twitch having people I care about in my home. Other than Hunt, no one has ever been here. Not my parents or my sister's. It was too far for my parents to get away from the farm, and my sisters had no interest in carting their families to the other side of the country.

Anyone else who has been here was nothing more than an acquaintance. Self-consciousness tightens my stomach now.

This house is so impersonal. There aren't photos or trinkets anywhere. It's meticulously clean to the point it could be considered clinical.

There's not an ounce of me inside these walls, and that's just sad.

"I had plenty to keep me awake," he chuckles before River swats his arm.

"One more time, Gray, and..." She doesn't have to finish the sentence before his spine snaps straight. His eyes flare wide, pleading with his wife to take it back. It's great seeing the guy's fun side alive again, but his wife has him by the balls, and I think that's even better.

"Uh, where can we put these?" Gray clears his throat, his words escaping at a pitch he probably hasn't hit since his pre-pubescent years.

"Follow me." Picking up Betty's suitcase again, she reaches for it, her fingertips grazing the back of my hand.

The electricity that has always sparked beneath my skin at her touch nearly brings me to my knees. *Fuck*, I've missed her, but what do I say? She looks so dejected, and after pushing her away so many times, I can't imagine she'll take me back again. Maybe she'll at least hear me out. Accept my apology. Even if she's not mine, I refuse to lose her in my life. The Hugheses are part of home for me.

"I can carry it," she whispers, avoiding my gaze.

"Not in my house," I retort, picking up the pace down the hall to the rear stairwell.

Gray remains at my heels as we ascend the stairs. This house is usually so quiet. Any noise comes from me. It's as unsettling listening to Gray and River playfully bicker about something I'm not paying attention to as it is inviting. That could have been Betty and me, but I fucked up.

"This is you," I point to one of the guest rooms on the opposite end of the house as my bedroom. From what I know about the two of them, they'll need the privacy, and so do I.

"Thanks, Nash," River pats my shoulder before entering the room. "I need a nap."

Then Gray grins my way and closes the door.

We haven't even turned away from the door before River giggles, and the sounds of them making out filter through the door.

"Come on," I wave Betty behind me.

She follows silently. I can't help but wonder what she's thinking. It's as if I can sense her coiled shoulders at my back, surely staring down the many doors we're passing. Three of them were additional guest rooms, but I lead her to the opposite side of the house. My end of the house.

There's one bedroom next to the master. The architect insisted we'd want a room for an eventual nursery since we were a young couple who would surely want a family. We'd barely unpacked our boxes before Katherine furnished the room as just another guest room. That was my answer.

We'd talked about kids, and though it wasn't something she wanted anytime soon, I had hope moving into our forever home might open her up to the idea more. The moment she decorated that room first, I knew it wouldn't, so I cast that dream aside and forgot about it.

The aesthetic is a match for the rest of the house, done up in dark shades and muted whites and creams. Once again, the term clinical comes to mind. It's decor you'd find at a hotel, not a home.

"I don't think you'll want to stay near them," I mutter, entering the room and dropping her suitcase on the bench at the end of the bed. "I'm across the hall if you need anything."

She still won't meet my stare, and it's breaking my fucking heart. Maybe if she just looks at me, I can apologize. I still want her. I want her more than I've ever wanted anyone, but she won't believe it, not after how I behaved.

The worst part is I didn't even realize I was doing something wrong until it was too late.

"I'm fine." Her voice is so small, so broken. My fingers twitch, wanting to reach out and hold her, but I can't. I lost that chance the moment I didn't open up to her.

In an instant, she turns her back to me, unzipping her suit-case. A dismissal that guts me worse than any of the words she's slung at me, calling me on my shit.

Retreating, I close the door behind me, jog down the steps, grab my keys, and leave the house.

I'm not going to survive in this house for three days with her ignoring me. I just can't. So I throw my truck in reverse, turn around, and bolt down my drive toward the gym. The burn is the only way I might stay sane.

CHAPTER 26

BETTY

The moment the first bead of sunshine peeks over the treetops, I'm out of bed and heading downstairs to the kitchen.

I assume Nash has coffee. If anyone's caffeine addiction could rival mine, it's that man. He'll have the good stuff, I'm sure of it. It was a commonality we found during our week of bliss. That black cup of instant energy is a necessity first thing, and not that typical grocery store brand nonsense. Exotic blends from South America are what get us going.

The pungent aroma of those energy beans hits me as I descend the stairs closest to the room I'd stayed in. Between thinking about Nash and River screaming through the night, sleep never found me. Just like the night before, I tossed and turned nonstop.

Shuffling into the kitchen, with the wood floors cold beneath my feet, my eyes meet Nash's. Those bright blue orbs nearly make me melt. His hair is messy, just like it had been the morning we woke up in the cabin. My eyelids fight to flutter closed so I can recall the memory of running my fingers through his locks while he peppered kisses along my jaw and collarbone.

"Morning," he grumbles, sipping from his mug. His voice is clear, absent of the gravel it held when I woke up in his arms.

The memories from that night and the following morning continue to filter to the forefront of my thoughts. He'd been so sweet. The way he'd held me and told me how beautiful I was first thing in the morning gave me the wildest butterflies. I'd tried to sneak off to brush my teeth and wipe the sleep from my eyes, but he'd only held me there, kissing me like it was the only thing he ever wanted to do in life.

Shaking my head, I suck in a deep breath.

You're okay, Betty. You can do this. Give it to him straight.

But when I meet his gaze again, I can't do it. The primary reason I came here was to confront him. *In or out?* Those were his options. Did he want to be with me or not? That's all I needed to know, and I can't even open my mouth to say good morning.

I shouldn't have come here. Nash was always a fantasy, and that's where he should have stayed. Ward may not have been forever for me either, but I'm surprisingly not heartbroken. He was the type of man my aunts always said I should find: one who wants you more than you want him.

Fail.

With an awkward wave, I reach into the glass cabinet, grab a mug, and pour myself a cup of coffee. The barstools at the kitchen island are the only place to sit unless I leave the kitchen altogether. But in a museum like this, I'm not sure how Nash feels about food and drinks in other rooms. So I have a choice: the seat beside him or the two across from him.

Choosing to put the four feet of marble between us, I slide onto the stool diagonal to his. Twisting the warm mug between my hands, I keep my focus toward the wall of glass at the back of his home. There's a massive patio area with furniture and a pool beyond that, surrounded by lush green grass and then a barrier of trees. It's stunning. The perfect distraction until Gray and River stumble into the kitchen, looking much more rested than Nash and me.

"Uh, good morning." Gray seems to word vomit hesitantly, unsure of what he walked in on. Only my heart is shattering as I sit here across from the only man I've ever truly wanted. "Did we interrupt something?"

"No!" Nash and I both practically shout in unison, our eyes meeting before we quickly look away. As if my eyes know it will hurt too much to look at his face and know he's fine, that he doesn't want me here, I only stare down into my mug.

"Right, uh... is there more coffee?" Gray runs his hands through his hair. The poor guy looks like a scared animal.

His hold on his wife's hand is firm enough that he could tug her and run as if he believes Nash and I will explode at any moment. We won't. We're barely acknowledging one another.

"Help yourself," Nash cocks his head backward.

River darts toward the pot, pouring herself a mug so full she'll need to sip it before she turns away.

As if he were ready and waiting, Gray snatches the mug from her. "No, you don't." The sound of his lips pecking her mouth causes my stomach to roll and my chest to ache. His grin only widens as River becomes more irritated, her eyes narrowing on his face.

"Gray, give that back to me. I'm dying," she whines. My brows shoot high. That's not like River. She makes demands. She holds her ground. Everything about that powerhouse of a woman is strong.

"Not a chance, baby." Gray's lips brush hers again, smiling widely while she pouts.

"Grayson Garrison, you're a cruel man," I chide him, assuming this is some cutesy couple moment I am getting to witness for the first time. Sipping from her mug, I expect he's seconds from handing her those precious contents of life back, but he doesn't.

"Exactly!" River's arms stretch out to the side, just to slap back into her thighs. Her antics only encourage him to laugh harder. "Just because there's a baby doesn't mean he has to police my caffeine," River whines before her hand claps over her mouth.

Yet another laugh barks free of Gray. River's outspoken nature often lets a truth slip, only to want to retract it. It made it easy for the two of us to become close so fast, especially since I'm an open book when I'm with her.

My eyes bulge wide as I stare at my best friend. "River, you're?" My gaze darts down to her stomach, then to her face, and finally to the goofy grin pulling at Gray's mouth.

"Uh, yeah. We are," River rubs her belly, smiling fondly at the man who captured her heart from day one. "Surprise."

Nash and I only stare at the pair of them. This moment must be even more awkward than what they stumbled in on. I'm overjoyed for my friends, but it was the last thing I expected. Though thinking back, every sign was there. No drinking at girls' night. The constant trips to the bathroom. Every absent stroke over her stomach and the way Gray doted on her more than necessary.

"Uh, well, congratulations," Nash hums, busying himself with pouring another cup of coffee.

"Thanks," Gray grins, guiding River to a barstool.

I immediately grab her hand, the two of us giggling. "I can't believe you didn't tell me!" The two of us gush over their good fortune, River telling me about the plans they already have for a nursery and how she's going to look for another doctor to hire at the practice and help at the rodeo.

And for a few minutes, all my issues melt away. All the heartbreak and the past. It's just my best friend and me celebrating this amazing moment together. River is going to be a mother. For some time, she told me it wasn't something she wanted right now. Her career was a priority, but eventually the tone changed. It changed to, *"When the time is right, Gray and I will have a family."* I can't recall when the shift actually happened, but I'm glad it did.

They deserve this happiness.

Absentmindedly, my hand rubs over my flat stomach. My past creeps in at the edges as Nash sighs heavily, Gray clapping him on the back awkwardly.

Those memories of the day I knew my relationship with Ryan was over filter back in.

Nash clears his throat, dropping his gaze to the counter, finally drawing my attention to him. "What are you talking about?" His voice is strained, as if he is fighting through his own inner turmoil. A pain so great it's too much to withstand.

"Let's try this again. What did we walk in on?" Gray questions, River's eyes darting between her husband and Nash as the tension grows.

Nash looks up at Gray, swallowing noticeably. "Why did y'all bring her?"

An audible gasp leaves Gray as if he's surprised by Nash's response. "She's running the B&B, so she's trying to learn everything about the rodeo. Figured it was a harmless trip." Gray shrugs, his brow scrunching low as if unsure what he's missing. It's then I know River hadn't said anything to Gray about what had happened with Nash and me.

"I'm too tired for this." Nash drops his head.

"Why? We all went to bed super early last night," River snickers, spinning on her stool.

"Um, River." My usual drawl drags out her name as the exhaustion weighs on me. "You and your husband were loud enough to keep the dead awake." It takes everything in me to keep my tone light. To pretend I'm not breaking into a million pieces hearing Nash say he doesn't want me here.

A barking laugh leaves Gray as River's complexion darkens. It's rarely easy to notice River's blush, but today you can't miss it.

"Way to call me out," River huffs.

"Someone had to tell ya the truth," I shrug, smiling around my mug before taking a large gulp.

The playful tone of the moment reminds me I'm here with my friends. I can handle these few days because they're here. It will all be fine.

"Truth, huh?" River smiles wolfishly.

There's that look. *No. No. No. She can't.* "River. Don't..." I plead.

"Nash, you should ask Betty why she wanted to come this weekend..."

Chapter 27

Nash

Breeding is the mating of animals to produce offspring. The same is true of humans. We fuck, we reproduce, and then there's a new generation waiting to follow in our footsteps.

Several key components comprise being a roughstock distributor. Breeding is one of those areas. It's always been the most interesting to me. I never had the patience to study science and the genetics behind what we do, but like the mathematical equations I've always used for my consulting, I thought there must be one for animals, too.

The right combination, in theory, should produce the desired offspring. With time and experience, you can identify the characteristics, traits, and pedigree that create the perfect athletes to train and then excel in their performances. The harder they buck, the better the score. That's the game. That's our responsibility.

I become someone else when I dive into work mode. The enormity of my responsibilities focuses me. Every thought aligns, and the pathway through the endless pieces of information guides my thought processes. It's all a puzzle for me to solve and determine the outcome. Is it desired or not? Is it what we're looking for? Are there other ways to capitalize on what's in front of us?

My list of analysis questions is endless. It's how my mind works and why I've been so successful.

We walked through several female cows, a heifer, and two bulls today. For two minutes, I lost my focus, my gaze locked on the profile of Betty's face as she asked intuitive questions about the bulls. Questions that made me wonder if she'd actually been studying up on all things rodeo, as she said. I never doubted her. However, I assumed it was more along the lines of an internet search. It's what most do, then throw on their boots and cowboy hats, pretending to be experts, just to make an ass of themselves when they say all the wrong things. Yet another reason I hate lingering around the locals after the rodeo. I'm stuck listening to their bullshit when all I want to do is sit in silence.

Those two fucking minutes were a movie on repeat in my mind the entire drive home. Three hours of Betty's voice and her scrunched nose and raised brow. Three hours of recalling how her jeans hugged her round ass and her toned arms flexed as her hands moved as she spoke. Torturous minutes of recalling how her sparkling brown eyes shone in the sun, and the way she and River giggled as they pet every cow they could get their hands on.

It had been such a reprieve not to obsess over her for a few hours, only to climb behind the wheel and think about nothing but her. I need to make this right between her and me. She may not want me back, but I can't exist in a world without her laugh or her friendship.

Gray and River disappeared to their room after dinner, River claiming she was exhausted. All it means is they're going to fuck until dawn, and I'm not sitting in my own house listening to it.

Wandering out to the back patio, the soft glide of the sliding door immediately drops me into the balmy night air. I used to sit out here a lot. It reminded me of the family farm: all the open land and fresh air. If I closed my eyes, I could pretend I was back there. I was home.

A heavy sigh leaves me as I shuffle toward the lounge chairs by the pool. I might be out here for a while, so I might as well get comfortable. Katherine insisted on these chairs because of a mesh technology that allowed them to mold to the body. To me, they were expensive for no reason, but again, she wanted them, so I gave them to her. That's a husband's job. We're supposed to provide.

Tapping do not disturb on my phone, I nearly launch it into the pool when I find Betty lying out in one of the chairs. "Betty?"

Her eyes remain trained on the sky above, mine tracking up at the midnight blue high above us. Every star seems to be out as if determined to illuminate the night sky. Maybe they are shining for the girl who has always treasured them more than anything. "Hey," she whispers.

That same disappointed tone of defeat coats that single word. Not once has Betty ever greeted me with a single word, and not so much as looked my way.

"Mind if I join you?" I ask slowly, lowering myself onto the lounge chair beside her.

Her shrug makes my brow scrunch low. Even when she was furious with me, she gave me more than this. Now I get nothing. How did I fuck us up so badly? "It's your house," she drones.

"Betty, look at me." My words escape softer than I would have imagined, especially when I'm this desperate for her eyes to meet mine. She hasn't looked at me since our awkward morning in the kitchen. I hadn't meant for her to hear what I said to Gray, but she did, and fuck did it destroy me to see her so heartbroken.

I should have known my words would be taken all wrong the moment they passed my lips. I wanted to know why they brought her here because I needed to know if there was hope for us. When I'd said I was too tired for this, I was referring to her cold shoulder. I was too exhausted to feel so shattered, though my actions were responsible for our current situation. I didn't mean to say anything negative about her.

Her head slowly turns toward me, her hands still crossed over her stomach. I can't read her expression as she just stares at me with those lifeless eyes. Not once have I ever seen her like this. The silence I always welcomed is stifling now. I need her to say something. Anything.

"Can I talk?" I ask nervously, running my palms together. Her brow arches high as her mouth sets into a straight line with her curt nod. This is up to me to bridge the gap. It's up to me to fix what I broke. "I'm sorry. The words aren't enough, but I am. It's just been me handling my shit for the past eight years, well, longer. I didn't think about including you because I've never had to include anyone, not even my ex-wife. There was nothing intentional about my distancing myself these past few weeks, and by the time I realized how it hurt you, I wasn't sure I could fix it."

"One call, Nash. Just one. That's all it would have taken."

"Baby, I'm sorry," I plead, but her glare keeps me from moving toward her. What I would give to hold her and make her believe I want her. That I need her because I do. "Betty, I want you. You know I do."

She angrily swipes a tear before it has a chance to snake down her cheek. "Do I?"

I can't take it anymore. I need to touch her. Shoving off my chair, I crouch beside her, her body bolting upright into a sitting position as if she's preparing to run. She keeps her thighs pressed tight together, mine straddling hers when I hold her in place. Cupping her cheek, my thumb swipes away another tear before I force her gaze to meet mine.

"You know I never wanted to stay in Cole County." Her head drops before she sniffles. "You would know that if you had ever just asked me what I wanted."

"Andromeda, look at me." Tucking my finger under her chin, I force her gaze to meet mine again. "Tell me what you want."

She only tears her chin out of my hold with a humorless huff. "It doesn't matter anymore. I'm leaving in the morning."

No. No, she can't leave. They're supposed to be here for another night. I was supposed to have another day to convince her I wanted this. "The hell you are," I snap, immediately clearing my throat, annoyed with myself for getting angry with her.

"My flight is first thing. I'm going to bed." She moves to stand, but I grab hold of her bare thighs, holding her in place.

"You're not leaving until you tell me what you want."

Our eyes lock, and I know this is my last chance. Whatever comes out of her mouth next will determine if I can still make her mine or if I lose her forever.

That is, if my heart doesn't give out waiting for her answer.

CHAPTER 28

BETTY

He ignored me all day. From the moment we left the kitchen, dressed, and met back in the foyer, not a single word. Not even when he held my door open for me to climb into the backseat of his truck. Not. A. Damn. Word.

Now he's out here demanding more from me? More, I'm not sure I have in me. How much more of myself do I have to give Nash before there's nothing left? Before, all I am is a shadow of the woman I've always known, but everyone else is just getting to meet.

Too many emotions course through me as I stare at his face. A face I've always known. Handsome with his straight nose and his thick umber hair that's usually styled but remains wild now as if he shook it after his shower and didn't touch it again. He'd looked the same the morning we woke up in the cabin together, wrapped in each other's arms.

His blue eyes draw me in. They, too, seem to swirl with emotion. I don't doubt that he cares about me. We've been in each other's lives for a long time because of my family, but how am I supposed to believe he wants me the way I need him to?

All he's done is run and push me away. No doubt I'm past the point where it would be considered respectable to give him another chance. I have to be. Right?

For my sake, I need to stay strong this time. Honest, sure, but no going back. I can't keep digging myself out of the pit of despair each time it gets to be too much for him.

His words echo through my mind. *"You're not leaving until you tell me what you want."*

He's had almost a year to ask me that question. It's been almost that long since I told him how I felt about him. Sure, I was drunker than an ox, but every word had been the truth. He'd told me exactly what I'd said during our week of bliss. Embarrassment flushed my cheeks as I hid behind my hands, but he'd only gently pulled them away and smiled down at me. *"I wouldn't have been ready to hear those words before,"* he'd whispered against my lips, before kissing each of my palms sweetly. *"But I'm glad I have now."*

Another tear slips free, replaying the moment. I'd believed him. I'd hung on every word and let my heart get carried away.

A long drag of air filters into my lungs as I press my eyes shut before meeting his again. "Part of me wants to hate you. I want to hate you for everything you've put me through. But I can't because it's not your fault that I let you." His lips part as if he's going to speak, but I only shake my head. "Part of me wishes I'd never met you. Because, Nash Donovan, if you'd never slept over at my house and found me outside under the stars with your kind smile and gesture, I would have never fallen in love with you." His fingers dig into my thigh, but I try to ignore it as my core tightens, knowing I am about to confess my worst want of all. "What's worse is a part of me still wants you to take me upstairs to your bedroom and make love to me."

Those vibrant blue eyes flare with heat, his sharp intake of breath causing me to look away. That hold tightens before he grips the point of my chin, forcing my gaze back to his.

"I can't do that." The words release as if he's straining to say them. My body jerks back, trying to pull away from him. I'm done. No more. I can't keep doing this to myself. "I can't make love to you, Andromeda. Not the first time. I've been waiting too long to have you."

My brain ceases to function... did he just—? My mouth opens and closes multiple times as I search for a response. A way to challenge him or encourage him to take me however he wants. I'm not sure which.

He tilts his head as if asking me to answer. Those eyes plead with me to say something. They've been doing that since he found me out here.

My fingers shake as I grab hold of Nash's. It's one night. I'm leaving in the morning, and then I can once again beat myself up for giving in to him so easily, but for now, I don't know how not to take advantage of this moment. I'm once again reminded that this is what I've always wanted—a real chance with Nash Donovan.

A hard swallow lodges in my throat before I can trust myself to speak. "Take me upstairs." His eyes search mine, darting back and forth as if in disbelief I'd just agreed. A wide grin stretches on his face before he pulls me to my feet, grabbing me behind my thighs and tossing me over his shoulder. "Nash!" I burst out laughing.

It makes no sense that I'm laughing as his fingers flex against my bare thighs. Not when the blood is rushing to my core and my head, splitting itself between the two body parts, both throbbing in tandem.

"I've wasted every other chance with you," he grunts. "I'm not tonight."

As if I weigh nothing at all, he marches through the house, up the stairs, and to the door at the end of our hall. He pauses for a moment. My only view is his toned ass and back, but I wish I could see his face. My heart seizes knowing this is the moment he backs away. He came to his senses before he even got me to his bedroom.

Dammit. Dammit. Dammit.

I press my eyes shut, cursing myself when he turns on his heel, kicks open my bedroom door with his toe, and then slams it shut with his bare foot.

Those rough palms run along my body as he slowly lowers me to my feet once again, watching my face as if he believes he might be dreaming. Cupping my cheeks, he lowers his mouth to mine. His lips are soft, almost questioning and tentative, as if he's not sure what's happening.

I haven't kissed him since just before the rodeo. It was nothing more than a spontaneous stolen moment in a random corner, just before Harper found me. He'd appeared out of nowhere, yanked me by the hand, and pinned me to the wall. His hard body pressed flush against mine as he kissed me stupid. What I would give to go back to that moment. A moment I was sure this was real.

A dark, smoky whiskey flavor coats his lips, wrapping my taste buds in a cozy blanket. A moan escapes me as his tongue swipes along the seam of my mouth, demanding entrance. He can have it. He can have everything if he's going to keep kissing me like this. Like he's starved, and I'm the only sustenance he'll ever need again. As if he wants me just as much as I want him. With that primal groan that just escaped him, I can almost believe he does.

Pulling away from my mouth, he breathes heavily, his forehead pressed to mine. "Listen to me. If I'm ever too much, you need to tell me, do you understand?" My eyes only search his, unsure of what he means. "Tell me you understand."

"Yes," I breathe, running my fingers over his cheeks and short beard. "Yes. Just please, Nash. Don't pull away again." The words are a plea, though fear of the past reminds me we always get to this point, and that's when he bolts. Those memories knot my stomach now.

Please *don't do this to me again.*

His fingers trail up my thighs, the tips slipping beneath the loose cutoff hem, before grazing the edge of my panties. My core contracts, remembering what it was like to have him almost touch me there, nearly taste me. "Andromeda, if you let me have you tonight, you're stuck with me forever."

Sweet baby cow on a stick. My insides sing in response to his words. My skin heating, and every muscle clenching in anticipation. This is it. The moment we've been waiting for the past twenty years.

"Nash, please. Touch me. Fuck me. Give me everything."

The scrape of his teeth over the column of my throat makes my toes curl against the plush area rug beneath my feet. "You asked for it."

CHAPTER 29

NASH

Fortune shines down on me tonight. I'm thanking the universe or the beings above, whoever made it so this amazing woman melted back into my arms.

When I asked Betty what she wanted, I never expected her to say she wanted to sleep with me. I also never expected her to come to me so willingly.

I'd planned to grovel. My old creaky knees were ready to ache for weeks from kneeling at her feet and begging if I had to. Then she said she was leaving, and I panicked.

She crashes her mouth back to mine, her tongue swirling inside my mouth. *Fuck*, I need her right now. I can explore her body later, once River and Gray are gone. There's no way in hell I'm letting her walk out my front door until we settle this shit. Sinking inside her won't solve the issues I created, but I can't wait anymore. I can't hold back.

For the first time in my life, I am crystal clear on exactly what I want. Beatrice Hughes. Period.

"Fuck," I groan as her nails drag over the thin cotton covering my chest. "Keep it up, and we won't make it the ten feet to that bed."

She only chuckles against my mouth, one hand reaching down between us to squeeze my throbbing cock. "I don't care," she breathes.

My palm snakes up the bottom of her shirt, feeling the expanse of her smooth stomach for the first time. Where Betty's legs and arms are toned as if she hits the gym as much as I do, her stomach is soft, the flesh giving under my touch. *Later, Nash. You can take your time later.*

Balling the fabric in my palm as I push it higher, I roughly tug her to me. "I'll buy you a new one." The tearing of cotton rips through the room, each strap of the tank top snapping free as I forcefully yank on the fabric. I've never torn clothing from a woman's body, but Betty does things to me I can't explain. I become feral.

The top pools at her hips, my finger immediately flicking open the button of her shorts. "Take them off," I nod to her. Her chest heaves with her panting breaths as she shimmies her shorts down her tanned thighs, stepping out of them. She shoves the remnants of her shirt over her hips, stepping out of it with one leg before kicking it off the ankle of the other.

Her eyes never leave my face. The two of us connected as if this had always been inevitable. Maybe we were. But, fuck if I care. She's mine now.

My eyes rake down her body. The closest I've ever seen her to naked was in a bikini a few years ago. It was summer, and a bunch of us were at the beach on the far side of Boulder Lake, celebrating Mrs. Crawley's birthday. I hadn't really looked at her then, but I am now.

Her pink nipples are taut and visible through her thin bra as her full breasts move with her exaggerated breaths. But, fuck, it's those panties that do me in. She'd been wearing the same type the first time I kissed her. The kind that leaves her ass cheeks exposed to my palms. This woman is absolute perfection.

Crooking my finger, she comes toward me, her eyes wide with lust. Tucking my finger into her tiny lace bra, I tug her against my body. Heat radiates off her skin, and it's taking everything in me not to throw her to the floor and drive into her.

Capturing her mouth with mine, I don't stop her as she undoes my belt, button, and zipper, shoving my jeans down my thighs. The two of us nearly fall over as I try to step out of the legs while she's attempting to tug my t-shirt up my body. Pulling my mouth from hers, I strip out of the rest of my clothing. The shirt, the remaining leg of my jeans, and boxer briefs. Each article lands somewhere in the room. It doesn't matter.

Our mouths meet again, her palms flat on my back, holding me close. Every muscle ripples beneath her touch. How is it possible to crave someone's skin against your own as much as you need to breathe?

Gripping behind her thighs, she groans into my mouth, hopping up to wrap her legs around my waist. Her giggle surprises me when I slam her back into the wall. Betty isn't supposed to like this rough and dirty. She's supposed to ask me to slow down or go easy on her, but she's right here with me. We're a frantic, hungry mess together, and that only makes my cock harder, that thick vein throbbing painfully.

Pulling her soaked panties to the side, I break my mouth away from hers. "I've never wanted someone so badly."

Her eyes flash with surprise before she swallows loudly, her swollen pink lips parting. "Then prove it."

Fuck. She has no idea what she just gave me.

Hope.

Hope for us and a future I didn't even know I wanted anymore.

My first finger slides through her swollen flesh, and fuck, I almost come all over her stomach. I'd barely felt her that first time, but now her arousal coats my fingers, and all I want to do is suck them clean before burying my face between her thighs.

"Nash, please," she whimpers, exposing the column of her throat to my tongue.

Sucking at the side of her neck, her hips buck into my palm. "Hold on, Betty."

Her fingers cling tighter to my hair, our stares locking. Pulling my fingers away from the heat of her pussy nearly brings me to tears. I wasn't done touching her, but I need to fuck her more. My body needs to feel her wrapped around us. Notching my cock at her entrance, I take one more breath before I push forward. Her head flies back, cracking against the wall, her mouth open as she moans against the intrusion.

"You're so damn tight. So fucking wet and all mine."

"Yes," she moans.

I hadn't even realized I had said the words aloud until she responded. I was sure they were in my head.

The number of times I've dreamed about this since she told me she'd been in love with me her whole life is unhealthy. But not a single dream or fantasy compares to the feel of her walls clamping around me. Each tiny push forward barely gains ground when all I want is to be buried inside her. Her pussy is my new favorite place. *Mine.*

"Nash," she moans, her fingers gripping my hair tight at the roots, as her hips try to flex back away from the pain.

"No, you don't. You're not getting away from me. Not now." I flick my tongue over her lower lip, placing an open-mouth kiss at the corner. "Not ever. Do you hear me?"

"Yes. Yes. More," she pants.

As much as I don't want to hurt her, the reins on my control are fraying with each tug at my hair and those delicious sounds escaping her mouth. Pulling back, I slam forward, burying myself in her. Her forehead smacks into my shoulder before her teeth sink into my flesh.

"Ahh," I groan against the pain. "Fuck, yes. Bite me. Mark me however you want, Andromeda."

Her tongue runs over the spot her teeth just sank into, sucking on me as I drive into her. I'm lost in her, our future flashing through my mind, making my hips pump harder. Her moans fill my ears before her gaze meets mine, her hand gripping the back of my head, pulling my face to her. "Harder," she demands.

A grin stretches across my face as I swing her away from the wall, dropping her on the bed. "On your hands and knees." There's no forgiveness in my tone, and she doesn't so much as flinch at my command.

With a teasing grin over her shoulder, she lines her knees up near the edge of the bed, her torso lowering as she falls to her elbows. Still, those wide brown eyes meet mine over her shoulder. Every bit of desire shines bright on her face. For a while, I convinced myself she didn't really want this. Why would she? But now I know for sure I was wrong. I had been from the beginning.

I can only stand there and stare before roughly tugging her panties down her thighs, allowing them to form a band above her knees. Unless she tears them, she's not going anywhere. She arches her back, exposing herself to me, and I nearly come all over the rug.

She's pretty and pink and glistening for me. Fisting my cock, her arousal coats my shaft, causing me to groan. Soon, it'll be a mixture of us all over me, and my cum filling her pussy. Maybe if luck is really on my side, it'll only take one time before she's pregnant.

Slow down, Nash. Savor the moment.

Running my palms over her bare ass causes her to wiggle her hips. "Be still, baby." I run my tongue over the curve of her right cheek, the silkiness of her skin making me groan loudly. Repeating the process on the left side, her body tenses as if fighting to obey. "That's my girl," I whisper against her skin.

Her arousal coats my fingers as I run them along her center, my thumb finding her clit, rubbing tight circles. Her body responds to me beautifully, as if eager to please as much as it wants to take.

Softly pressing against her lower back, her ass rises a little higher. I give no warning as I line myself up at her entrance and slam home. My pace is torturous—a pounding thrum to match my racing heart. My name on her lips is like a chant, serving as all the fuel I need to claim her as mine.

She fists the comforter, her knuckles turning white with her tight grip. We have only moments. Moments before I send her over the edge. Moments before the mixture of the two of us fills her pussy. Fuck, I hope she's not on birth control.

"Let go. Give me everything," I grunt, gritting my teeth to hold back my release. No fucking way I am coming before this woman. Not tonight, not ever.

"Nash," she pants, fighting to glance at me over her shoulder as I relentlessly pound into her.

I don't even get out another word before she comes undone, shouting my name loudly enough that Gray and River surely heard it if they're still awake. Her walls flutter around me, her breathing filling my ears. Still, I don't stop drawing out her pleasure, keeping her just high enough that her body refuses to relax around me.

Sweat cascades from my temples and down my back as I fight the urge to come. I'm not done. I want more. This can't end. My hips jerk wildly twice more before that familiar tingle hits the base of my spine, and I spill inside her.

An entire lifetime of the two of us flashes before my eyes as rope after rope shoots inside her. There's no way I'll ever be done with her, not after this.

Fighting to catch my breath, I pepper kisses along her spine. "Just give me a minute, and then we'll take a shower."

She only hums as if words are too much of a challenge for her to put together.

Slipping free of her, a grin pulls at the corners of my mouth. She's filled with my cum. It's a beautiful sight. She rolls onto her back, her legs falling wide open with her panties somehow only hanging off one ankle now. "Mmm," I hum, scooping her up in my arms. "That pretty pussy looks beautiful overflowing with my cum." She only grins in response, her cheek falling to my chest, but she doesn't open her eyes, her breathing evening out. "Wake up, Andromeda."

"No," she groans with a lazy smile curving her swollen lips.

"Yes. What kind of man would I be if I didn't make sure my woman went to bed satisfied and clean?"

"A man who lets me die a happy woman."

Kissing the tip of her nose, I only chuckle as I carry her across the hall. This is going to be the quickest shower we've ever had. I need to be in bed with her, wrapping her in my arms, while she snores against my chest. We were perfect like that, and we will be again.

CHAPTER 30

BETTY

The warmth of someone else's skin makes my cheek sweat as I groan awake.

Arching my back, my entire body aches. *Geez*, I really had sex with Nash Donovan last night. *I. Had. Sex. With. Nash. Donovan.*

My mind doesn't know whether it wants to sit in stunned silence or cheer in victory. How had we gone from not speaking to sex? How does that happen?

Rolling all the way onto my side, it seems surreal to watch him. I've never seen him as relaxed as when he sleeps. He'd woken before me at the cabin, so I hadn't gotten this moment to appreciate his handsome face. The dark hair and short beard give him such a rugged appearance, especially with the proud, straight nose dotted in freckles from the sun.

Time seems to stop as I curl into his side and stare. I'd finally gotten everything I had always wanted. Nash said all the things I've been waiting to hear for what seems like a lifetime. Then it hits me, the wave of nausea, causing me to scoot to the opposite edge of the bed.

We'd had sex without protection. It's not diseases I'm worried about, but the fear of getting pregnant. I'd been on birth control then, too. Somehow, luck wasn't on my side, though.

Slipping out of bed, I rifle through my suitcase searching for clothing. Underwear, bra, sweats, t-shirt. I'll look crazy, but I need to get to town. This can't happen. Not again.

Panic has my heart racing. Every breath escapes as a wheezing pant, remembering what happened last time I'd let emotions get away from me. I'd lost everything. My entire life devolved into nothing as I sank into myself.

"Betty," Nash groans behind me. "What are you doing?"

I startle, jumping away from my suitcase like a child caught with their grubby hands in the cookie jar. My eyes become saucers as they bounce around the room. "Um, can I borrow your truck? Please." My voice quivers, the words barely escaping between my uneven breaths.

"You're not leaving," he groans again, those cobalt eyes finally focusing on my face.

I'm not sure what he sees, but he jumps out of bed instantly, marching over to me. His muscles flex as his hands cup my face. Tucking my lips into my mouth, I fight to keep my gaze focused on the wall behind him and not his naked form in front of me. *Don't. Look.* "Your truck? Can I—" I can barely voice the question again.

"Where are you going?" he questions, ducking so I have to meet his stare.

This wasn't something I ever wanted anyone to know. I've carried it alone for the past seven years. Only my mom knows, but we've never talked about it again after that day. I told her not to ask me how I was doing, and she has honored that.

"I just. Um, I need to go into town."

"Okay, I'll take you." His eyes scan the room for his clothes, finding them scattered around the floor before he slips them on.

"Nash, I don't want you to come. Just..." I drag in a shaky breath, fighting back the tears burning behind my eyes as my stomach continues to churn. "Never mind, I'll just call a cab."

Taking a wide arc around him, he reaches for me, just catching my fingertips. "I don't know what's going on here, but I need you to tell me. Did I hurt you? Was it what we did?"

That first tear slips free as my chin falls to my chest. Resolve settles in my gut. If I want something real with Nash, this isn't a secret that can die with me.

"You might want to sit down," I sigh, pulling free of his hold to sit on the edge of the unmade bed.

He slowly lowers himself beside me, a hand resting on my thigh in reassurance.

"I don't know if you ever knew about my last long-term relationship. Ryan and I were together for years, and things were great. I thought he'd be the man I married." Nash's fingers tighten on my thigh with my words, but I keep going. "Um, there's really no good way to put any of this, but I ended up pregnant. I was on birth control, so I was surprised, but I lost myself after that." The knots in my stomach tighten. Having to relive those feelings all over again with the man of my dreams next to me hurts so much more than I ever thought it would. I've never talked about this. Never said the words out loud, and now that I am, I wish I could put it all back in the box tucked away at the back of my mind. "I sat with the information for a few days, realizing that though I've always wanted kids, I didn't want them with him. It was impossible for me to reconcile that I thought I'd marry the guy, but didn't want to have children with him. To make a long story short, I never told him. My mother went with me to a clinic. I had an abortion, and I've never told anyone until now. It's a fear that has stuck with me and often keeps me from sleeping with anyone."

Nash pulls me into his side, wrapping his arms around me before kissing the top of my head. "Baby, I'm so sorry."

"It's the past..."

"Clearly it's not," he retorts, causing me to flinch at his words.

Pulling out of his hold, my gaze meets his. There are no judgments or adverse feelings there. Just acceptance and something deeper. An emotion that reminds me of how I've felt about him all these years, but I shake the image free.

He can't...

He doesn't...

Grabbing hold of his hand, I take a deep breath before divulging the rest of my confession. "I just freaked a little realizing we had sex without protection."

"Betty, I."

"No," I shake my head. "I didn't freak out because I didn't want a baby." Meeting his gaze once more, my vision clouds with tears. Just as the first one falls, he wipes it away. "You're the only man I've ever envisioned a family with, and I don't know what last night was. I don't know if you meant the things you said or how long before you pull away again. That's terrifying, Nash. So rather than allowing myself to get lost in the fantasy of us once more, I was gonna go into town, buy a Plan B, and never say a word to you about it." Averting my gaze, shame washes through me. "I know that's shitty. I still feel horrible for not telling Ryan all those years ago, but it took me too long to crawl out of the pit of depression that it caused. But with you, if you walked away, I wouldn't survive another one."

A rough palm slides over my cheek before Nash's lips brush mine. The kiss is soft, communicating so much more than words ever could. He doesn't deepen it or consume me the way he had the night before. It feels like he's telling me to trust in his words. To trust in us and what we might become.

"Listen to me when I say this," Nash's voice lowers as his eyes lock with mine. "I hope I got you pregnant. I meant what I said. This, us," he points between our chests, "is happening. You're mine, Beatrice Hughes. Most would say for as long as you'll have me, but that's not good enough. You're mine no matter what. Good, bad, angry, or filled with joy. I've let you go over and over again, and I won't do that again. You need a break from me? Pick another room, go shopping with your friends, I don't care, but this is happening."

Dropping my head again, I only nod. I don't know how to respond to that. Every part of me wants to believe the conviction in his words, but my experience with him tells me it's only a matter of time.

He will walk away again.

But for today, maybe I can live the fantasy. For now, I can enjoy it until I wake up from the dream, and I'm once again devastated.

Placing a chaste kiss on his mouth, I force a smile. Betty is good at pretending. She can do it now, too. "If that's true, then I would suggest you feed me."

CHAPTER 31

NASH

My body vibrates with the purest joy. I've never felt like this in my life, not with any accomplishment or even marrying Katherine. I've never felt so at peace as listening to Betty cackle at my kitchen island, drinking coffee in her bare feet, while I cook enough to feed the entire town.

"I'm surprised you actually know how to cook," she snickers, filling her mug for the third time.

Grabbing hold of her wrist, I pull her body flush against mine. "You're gonna drink all my coffee, Andromeda." She only shrugs, tucking the newly filled mug to her chest. "You're lucky you taste better than any coffee bean in this world," I snap my teeth at her, releasing her so I can swat her ass.

She yelps, scurrying away, sliding back onto the barstool closest to me.

We're a pair of regular caffeine addicts. The thought makes me chuckle aloud as I shake my head. Flipping another pancake out of the pan, she whoops as if I just completed some herculean feat.

This is what I imagined relationships were supposed to be like. Fun and full of laughter, doing the mundane tasks of daily life. Puckering my lips in her direction, hoping she'll give me the hundredth kiss since we came down to the kitchen almost an hour ago, she snorts. But she's up off the stool again, never releasing her mug, kissing my mouth, only to giggle louder as she tries to pull away while I pepper more all over her face.

"Nash, stop," she snorts. "You're gonna make me spill my coffee."

"Then stop moving and let me kiss you as much as I want."

She only snorts again, finally getting out of my hold. "You're impossible when you're all happy 'n stuff."

Her comment makes me pause, wondering if everyone thinks I'm unhappy. I'm not the type to care about what others think. But I've never actually thought about it. It's all streamlined focus for me. Work, business, gym, work some more, family. With such an even-keeled lifestyle, I never thought anyone would think I was unhappy with the life I had chosen.

I was. I am. But now that I have Betty, the priorities and lifestyle will change. And I want that. It was a life I expected Katherine and I would find at some point, but we never did. We were only roommates by the end. There was never that passionate sort of love that sets the blood in your veins on fire or makes your heart race a million beats a minute.

"Nash!"

"Hmm," I hum, not realizing Gray had been calling my name. "Oh, hey. When did you two get down here?"

"Long enough for River to fight me over the coffee again," Gray groans.

A chuckle leaves me as I pull the last strips of bacon from the pan and drop them on the serving plate. "Well, perfect timing. Y'all should eat something before you get on the road."

"I'm starving," River rubs her stomach, not hesitating to grab one of the plates I set out, and piling it high. Even before we found out she was pregnant, the woman ate plenty. Gray was happy to tell us all about their life together, and from time to time, she'd bring him lunch, so we all got to witness it firsthand.

We each load up our plates, our conversation revolving around the cows we saw the day before. Once again, Betty surprises me with her insightful questions, my hand squeezing her thigh with each one. It was the only way I would keep from devouring her mouth indecently in front of our friends.

"Okay, enough beating around the bush," River drops her fork, rubbing her stomach.

"What's going on here?" she points a finger between Betty and me. It's a fight to keep a wide grin from pulling at my cheeks. Squeezing her thigh once more, I allow her to answer in a way that she feels comfortable.

Bringing her mug to her lips, she takes several large gulps before answering. "We just talked last night, and we're good."

"Thank goodness. The tension was so thick between y'all I thought we were going to suffocate yesterday." Betty winces at Gray's words, but doesn't pull away as I link my fingers through hers beneath the island top.

River slides off the stool with a heavy sigh, her eyes meeting Betty's. "Okay, well, let's go get packed."

Betty stays silent, her eyes darting between Gray and River before meeting mine. "I, um. Well, Nash invited me to stay for a few more days." I hate that she sounds unsure, as if she expects me to take back my words. Though I hadn't offered, I'd practically begged her for ten minutes before she gave me an inch. *"I'll consider it,"* she'd whispered.

"Why?" River questions as her features scrunch.

My heel bounces off the stool foot bar, fighting myself. I want Betty to feel comfortable sharing what happened between us. And suddenly I understand what it means to be loved loudly. I need her to feel that way about us.

"Well, Nash and I are trying," she says, tiptoeing around us. I can't blame her. Her insecurities stem from me, and it's up to me to fix those. "So, we're going to hang out for a few more days. I'll fly back with him on Wednesday."

My insides soar. My entire being figuratively nuzzles on cloud nine.

"You two?" Gray's eyes gape in our direction. "It's about time. Maybe you'll stop being so damn grouchy now."

"Pot calling kettle," I grunt. He only frowns in my direction as if confused by my comment. "You were miserable to be around most days until you met River. So, River, thank you for your service."

She only snorts before locking eyes with her friend again. "Betty, if you're sure..." Her words linger in the air. Confirmation that my girl has been honest with her best friend about what I put her through. Shameful moments I wish I could erase from their memories, but also understand I wouldn't be here without them.

"I'm sure," Betty nods. "We'll get dinner when I get back."

A glint shines in both of their eyes. Dinner surely means a gossip session between the two. It'll be their opportunity to chat openly about River's pregnancy and what happened between us.

River and Gray disappear hand in hand, Betty staring after them with a fondness I hope is her wish for us.

Once they're out of sight, I pull her between my legs, wrapping my arms around her waist. "So what are we going to do for the next few days?" I chuckle, kissing her shoulder.

She doesn't answer, shrugging before she wiggles out of my hold. The moment she reaches for our plates, I stop her, kissing her knuckles. "Not in my kitchen."

Her eyes roll, ignoring me as she dumps all our mugs in the sink. She scrapes each plate clean, washes them, and then loads them into the dishwasher. Knowing I won't win this one, I wipe down the counters before returning the butter and syrup to their rightful places.

Every second feels so natural, roaming and cleaning the kitchen as a pair. Is that what our lives could become? The two of us living this domestic experience where all I can think about is us finishing our chores so we can christen every surface.

My gaze roams across the expanse of the space. The kitchen. The family room. Even the patio and pool area outside. Each location is untouched and waiting for us to make it our own.

Sliding up behind Betty, I press in against her, that smile as welcoming as her ass wiggling against my crotch. "Careful," I warn her. "We might end up giving our friends a show they aren't prepared for."

She snorts, leaning into me. "Payback for keeping us awake two nights ago."

Kissing the side of her neck, she tilts her head, giving me better access. Her skin is warm against my mouth, my tongue tracing along her jugular before she giggles, ducking away from me. "Okay, calm down. I'm almost done, so why don't you show me something you like to do?"

Her body spins to face me, my arms caging her in against the sink. The moment is so similar to the first night I kissed her at her parents' house. It seems like eons ago, though it was only a little over three months. I could say that's when I started feeling something for her, but that's not true. I watched and listened and fought myself from that night at the bar almost a year ago.

I'd been the one to ask her to dance, her arms looped around my neck as I held her respectfully close. She'd been three sheets to the wind, so I was looking out for her. There were too many men in there that night with eyes on her, and what type of friend would I be to the Hughes family if I'd let her get taken advantage of?

The beat was a slow lull, our bodies swaying at the center of the dance floor, when those beautiful brown eyes locked with mine. *"You know, Nash, you're the man of my dreams. I've thought about you every day since I was ten years old. Do you know what it's like being in love with someone for so long and they don't know?"* she snickered to herself, then, before her fingers sank into my hair. *"Well, now you do, I think. Yeah, I'm in love with you, Nash, and there's no one I want more than you."*

There have been countless nights I replayed that interaction. There was no good response at the time. She was my buddy's younger sister. A woman eight years younger than me. Her family had been as much of parents to me as my own, sometimes more so over the years. There were excuses after excuses for why we would never work. Countless reasons we didn't make sense.

I recited those excuses day after day. I made them part of me so that maybe then I could believe that Betty's confessions didn't make me see her differently. That her stepping over the line didn't open my eyes to the beautiful woman in front of me, erasing the sweet, fun-loving little girl who loved constellations and staring up at the stars in the middle of the night.

Leaning in closer, my mouth hovers over hers. "Do you have any gym clothes with you?"

Her brow cocks. "Gym? Clothes?" The way she voices those two words, I'm not convinced she's ever set foot inside a gym. "I'm not the cardio type." Her cute nose wrinkles as if disgusted by the thought.

Brushing my lips over hers, my words are barely above a whisper. "Neither am I, at least not the type you're thinking."

CHAPTER 32

NASH

Sundays have always been my day off from the gym. Most of the time I'm traveling, but it's also just a reset day—cleaning, laundry, and administrative work.

I usually spend my hours on the couch reviewing the pending consultations and contracts that are coming down the line. Once I've read through each file long enough that my temples are throbbing, I move on to the roughstock. That's several more hours of obsessing over the stats and every performance. Year after year, we've had nationally ranked bulls in the NFR and PBR, and I'm not about to ruin that legacy for our family's business.

The clank of weights fills my ears as I open the door for Betty. The possessive man in me needs to stake his claim as the guy at the front desk looks up and smiles at her. Weaving my fingers through hers, I'm likely squeezing a little too tight, but she only squeezes back, following me into the belly of the space.

"What's your favorite body group?" I ask, searching for a good spot for us to start.

"On you?" she quirks a brow, drawing out my laughter.

There's nothing that makes me happier than her ogling my body. The rake of her gaze over my frame and every chiseled muscle I've worked my ass off over the years to build and then maintain makes my cock twitch in excitement. My woman is free to stare at every part of me.

Squeezing her hand again, I only shake my head. "As much as I'd love to have that conversation with you, I was thinking more of training today. Legs, arms, core, glutes?" Heat flares in her stare with that last suggestion. The need to adjust myself, remembering what she'd looked like last night, ass in the air as I licked each cheek, causes my hips to shift, trying to roll out the discomfort.

"Don't you fitness freaks have schedules or something?" she quips with a grin.

Betty Hughes might be the death of me.

"You asked for it." Dragging her behind me, our first stop is the hack squat machine. I always start with the exercises I love most, so I'm forced to push harder as the workout continues. It's a method that helps me strengthen my discipline, reinforcing the work ethic I've applied to everything I've done throughout my life.

Betty pushes through every exercise like a pro. Not once does she shy away from telling me the weight is too heavy or too light, or asking questions to help with proper form. I'd never considered sharing this part of my life with a partner. Other than Hunt, and when I played sports, the gym was a place just for me. It served as the clarity I needed when I couldn't find it elsewhere or didn't have the time to get lost in the grind of ranch work.

I'm on my last set of Bulgarian split squats, my thigh trembling as if I'm made of nothing more than Jello, when my eyes meet hers. Her skin is flushed and drenched in sweat. Not once did she try to pretend it wasn't there or wipe it away to make herself look more put together. The orderly bun she'd arrived with sits lopsided now, and loose strands stick to her neck and temples.

"Three more, Nash. Let's go," she claps.

A second wind rarely hits me when I've pushed this hard. It's all sheer will and mindset that force me to complete the set. But today, having those brown eyes focused on me, something shifts. This, Betty, a partner, is what I've been missing all this time.

It never seemed as though I was going through the motions of life before, but maybe I was. I did my job and kept my company alive, because who would let it fail? But for the first time, I'm questioning whether I even like it.

The same is true of the responsibilities I have to the distribution business. I fulfilled my obligations. The dutiful son learned the ins and outs because I was told one day it would all be mine. One day, I would find myself back in Cole County, bound to a legacy I never asked for.

"That's my guy," Betty lightly ruffles my hair as I slump onto the bench. I only wince up at her with a half grin and one eye squinting closed to keep the sweat from blinding me.

"I don't know how you were never a cheerleader," I grunt.

"Too dainty for me." In a swift motion, she inhales a deep breath, lifting one of my weights, her back leaning as she waddles to return it to the rack. I follow with the second one before wiping down the bench and snatching my bag from the floor. Draping an arm over her shoulders, she rests her head against my side. It's perfect. What I would give to start every morning like this.

"You did great today," I praise her, keeping her tight to my body as we exit the glass front doors out into the scorching sun.

"I've never worked out like that, but I like it. All I've really done is self-defense classes with Beckett. He insisted when I started working at the bar," she drones as if annoyed her brother cares too much.

"I remember. He told me when I was home to help my dad one weekend. We just want our Betty Minor safe," I chuckle, opening the truck for her.

Without so much as a wince, she slips into the cab, buckling her belt. Unlike my younger woman over there, my knees creak and my ass burns as I jump into the driver's seat. Becoming an athlete from a young age and continuing through college took a toll on me. I've rebuilt myself stronger over the years, but these joints and muscles still like to remind me I'll be forty-one in a few months.

Pulling out of the lot and onto the road, I hesitate to bring up our conversation from this morning. I meant every word, but I also need her to know that whatever she wants to do with her body will always be her choice. It doesn't matter what I want in that regard.

Placing a hand on her thigh, her gaze tracks up to me. "Did you still want to stop at the pharmacy?" My pulse races waiting for her answer. I realize I don't know this part of her or how she'll respond. It'll take time for me to grasp how much of a toll that time in her life really took on her. In time, I hope she'll open up to me about that. I can't imagine carrying that all alone for years.

"Do you want me to?" Her voice is small, but those eyes never leave my face. I can feel them boring into the side of my skull, waiting. Nervous.

"Baby," I grab her hand, kissing her knuckles, never taking my eyes off the road. "It's your choice. I meant what I said this morning. It may seem like I just said all of it in the heat of the moment, but I didn't. I've had months to process my feelings for you and to come to terms with my own insecurities, so when I say I want everything with you, I mean it."

She's quiet for what seems an eternity. Slowing my breathing, I focus on the feel of her palm against mine. In time, my pulse seems to pace with the idle swipe of her thumb over my knuckles, the sensation so soothing, I wonder if she's about to blow up my world with her words.

"Then I'm good. We can go home."

Without another word, we take off down the road. The tires fly over the pavement as if I'm competing in a NASCAR race, and home is the finish line. Traffic seems to be against me, though. Traffic that may be common on Sundays, but I wouldn't know since I stay at my house, and more often than not lately, I've been home.

Home.

Cole County, not Montana.

When did I stop thinking of Montana as home, too?

The obvious turning point won't present itself to me. There was before, and now. That's all I know.

Betty's fingers squeeze mine again as I turn onto the dirt portion of my drive. I hope she'll be comfortable alone here with me. She'd had the buffer of her best friend before, and I have no doubt River would chop off my balls if I'd hurt Betty again.

Throwing the truck in park, I'm moving slower than I'd like, edging around the hood to open her door. Taking my hand, she slides out of the cab, once again linking our fingers. It's indescribable how her touch undoes me.

It's a cross between an ongoing storm raging inside me that her light can silence, while simultaneously feeling as though I'd been dead, and she brought me back to life. It's a conundrum I can't figure out. How can both be true at the same time? How can Betty be everything I never knew I needed and all the things I stopped wanting when I found comfort in the mundane with my previous marriage?

"Let's get a shower, I'll order us some food, and we can just have a lazy day, okay?"

She pulls me to a stop, her hands on either side of my torso. "If you have work to do, you don't have to entertain me. I have a book with me."

"How did you know I work on Sundays?"

Her head tilts as if confused by my question. Our bodies drift closer, her front flush against mine. "I've been in love with you for twenty years. I know everything you try to hide, because I hid so I could know you without anyone noticing." Her words overpower me, emotions coursing through me so rapidly I can't parse them. Pressing up onto her toes, her lips brush mine before gripping my hand and leading me upstairs. She releases me as we come to her bedroom door. "I'll meet you downstairs," she whispers before slipping inside.

Racing into my bedroom, I grab an armful of clothes before elbowing back into hers. "What are you doing?" she gasps, her sweaty t-shirt discarded on the floor and her thumbs hooked into the waistband of her leggings.

Sweat darkens her hot pink sports bra, my tongue flicking across my lower lip, wanting to lick every drop off her skin.

"Putting my stuff in the drawers," I answer, willing my cock to relax. I should feed her before I fuck her again.

"Uh, why? You have a room."

My head bows as I lean over the dresser, my clothes a haphazard pile in front of me that will make me twitch in annoyance later.

"Because, Andromeda," I say slowly, turning to face her so she knows I mean every word. Her lips part, tracking my expression, but she doesn't come to me. "The only memories in this room are with you."

CHAPTER 33

BETTY

Two days locked away with Nash in his Montana mansion was just as blissful as our week together. More painful, too. Our mornings kicked off with the gym, where he pushed me past limits I didn't know I had, followed by working side by side on his couch.

Hunt had called him to come out to see a client, but he told his best friend to handle it. It wasn't our first argument, but definitely a point of contention for a solid twenty minutes before he hugged me into his chest and explained himself. It was the first time he had really opened up about his marriage and how they had become two ships passing in the night. There was no desire to go out of his way to spend quality time. If it happened, it happened. It was that simple.

He didn't want that for us. Hearing his fears and desires laid out in that way made me see him in a different light. Nash had always been a hard worker. He'd always put business and family first, but never his wife. There's no way I would have known that, but now I do, and I can understand why he is so adamant not to do that to us. It also explains his actions so much more when he disappeared for a few weeks. It doesn't excuse his actions, but at least I can let go of that pain.

But my own insecurities still linger. I don't want to be the one who holds him back or forces him into a lifestyle he hasn't chosen for himself.

It's been about an hour since he dropped me at my apartment, promising he'd be back after visiting his parents. His mom was finally home from the hospital. He'd asked me to come, intent on us spending every second together. But I saw the weariness in his stare. The worry and the preparation needed to steel himself for whatever he might find. I thought it might be best for him to spend time alone with his family.

But mostly, I'm not sure I'm ready for our families to know about us.

The past few days have been an absolute dream. My muscles have never been so deliciously sore. Weights and sex might be my favorite combination for the start of each day. More importantly, getting to witness this open-door version of Nash and having him doting on me and holding me was everything I've ever wanted.

Still, our past hovers like a dark cloud. It's impossible not to wait for the other shoe to drop. We'd found our island before, only for him to disappear on me. I understand there were reasons, but I can't handle a fourth time, especially not now that we've had sex, not now that he's said all the things I've always wanted to hear from him.

Tossing my suitcase onto the bed, I'm quick to unpack, throwing the clothes in the washer and my toiletries back in the bathroom.

Unfortunately, I've been called in to work at the bar tonight, so I don't have a lot of downtime. Wednesdays are always mid-week inventory before the weekend rolls around, which means I won't be out of there before three in the morning.

The buzz of my phone has me spinning in a circle, attempting to find where I'd left the blasted device. Finally spotting it under the corner of my open suitcase, I chew my inner lip, reading the text.

River: *Good? Bad?*

I hadn't talked to her much since she and Gray left Sunday morning. We agreed that I would deliver every detail when I returned, but part of me wants to keep these past few days with Nash between us just a little longer.

> **Me:** *Very good!*

> **River:** *Good. I can tell Fester to stand down.*

Letting out the most unladylike laugh, I place my phone on the dresser, continuing to unpack my suitcase before shoving it in the closet.

My phone buzzes again, my head shaking, knowing River is going to be relentless until we have dinner tomorrow night.

But my breath hitches when I see the name on my screen.

> **Nash:** *I miss you already. Mom is doing much better. I'm going to stay here until 4 and then I'll swing by to pick you up.*

> **Me:** *I'm glad. Tell your parents hi for me.*

> **Me:** *I'm working at the bar tonight. You can see me tomorrow.*

> **Nash:** *I'll pick you up at 4. Don't let me get there and you're already gone.*

> **Me: *You're impossible.***

> **Nash: *No I'm yours.***

Crushing my phone to my chest, those teenage butterflies fill my stomach.

"This is it, Betty," I say to no one, spinning in my spot before collapsing backward onto the mattress.

Excitement for the future courses through me, but that tiny seed of doubt lingers. How long will it last?

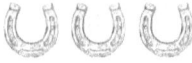

"Joe, this is the last one." I flash a wide grin at my favorite regular. He's been working at Boulder Ranch since before I was born. How the man continues to move the way he does is beyond me. Like Old Man Wilber, he's doing things he has no business doing at his age, but he also has no one left to care for him. He had no children, and his wife died years ago. No one has the heart to make him retire.

He only grunts, downing half his mug of beer in a few gulps. "You're no fun." Rolling my eyes, I swat at him with my towel. "Right, Donovan? She ain't no fun!"

Nash grins from his spot at the end of the bar. As promised, he was standing at my front door at two minutes to four. There was no dissuading him from driving me to the Thirsty Pony or telling him to leave, and I'd catch a cab home. He wasn't leaving and has stayed parked on that bar stool watching me and every man who has spoken to me.

He'd started with a beer, then had a second before switching to water, and it's only eight.

"My girl is a lot of fun," Nash winks before nodding his chin toward Joe.

"Your girl, huh? Her daddy know you're robbin' the cradle?"

"Joe," I scold, swatting him again. "I'm thirty-three."

"So. That Donovan boy could be your daddy." I burst out laughing as he continues to mumble to himself when I place a glass of water in front of him.

"Your math is a little off, but thank you for the concern."

Turning my back to both men, my stomach rolls. I hate that Joe brought up our age difference. Nash had admitted that was one of the original reasons he'd tried to keep his distance, in addition to being Beckett's friend, feeling like a Hughes child in a way, and not being able to give me a steady life.

He's given me the truth, thinking it would put me at ease, and it partially has. It's also given me a specific list of fears to cling to. Reasons that Nash will walk away because his insecurities are stronger than the feelings he has for me.

The hours pass, my shoulders burning from the gym as much as slinging drinks at a packed bar. Wednesday nights are always busy like this. There's no good reason for it, unless it's amateur night at Boulder Ranch, which it's not tonight. But it's still summer. We'll be an attraction until the kids go back to school and the holiday season rolls around.

By the time the last patron exits through the front door, waving goodbye, I'm dead on my feet. But the work isn't done. With me being the only bartender on tonight, inventory will take me at least an hour, and that's if the backroom is organized. These young guys Jim hired aren't always the best.

Snapping the lock closed on the front door, I turn to find Nash rounding up empty bottles and glasses off the tables. He doesn't say a word as he effortlessly slips through the space, tossing trash and wiping down every surface.

With a sigh, I get to work, focusing on shutting down behind the bar before I head back and do inventory. The faster I get it done, the quicker I can snuggle into my pillow and sleep until noon.

"What can I do next?" he breathes heavily next to me, his warm breath caressing my bare neck.

It had been another blistering hot day, and I couldn't tolerate more than a tank top. When the bar is packed, the air conditioner is pretty much worthless, but now it blessedly cools my skin.

"Inventory," I groan, wrapping my arms around his neck with a lazy grin.

Strong hands massage the muscles along my arms, his eyes sparkling in the dim light. Mischief dances there, my core tightening, unsure of what he's thinking.

Before I can speak again, his mouth closes over mine. My fingers tug at his neck, pulling him closer to me, lost in the feel of his lips and body. Our mouths slant, deepening the kiss, before the tip of his tongue teases across the seam of my lips, asking for entrance. Entrance, I'll always happily give him.

I'm so wrapped up in Nash, I hardly notice he's already undone my belt, button, and zipper on my jean shorts. "If we're gonna be here another couple of hours, I'm not gonna be able to wait that long to taste you."

"Nash," I whisper my warning. "We can't... here." My eyes dart around the space as if someone is hiding under the tables and will pop out to catch what we're about to do.

"We can, and I will," he smirks. Yanking his shirt over his head, the muscles of his torso flex. My nails run down his chest, reveling in the feel of his solid pecs and every ridge of his abs rippling beneath my touch.

He lays his shirt out on the bar countertop before hoisting me to the edge, yanking my shorts down my legs, and then scooting me back just far enough I won't slide off.

"Nash," I whine. It was meant to be another warning, but every nerve ending is alive as he runs his hands up my outer thighs. I've never done anything like this in a public place. Definitely not my place of work.

But my body hums with the anticipation of having his mouth on me. My core pulsing, remembering what it feels like for his tongue to swirl around my swollen nub and sink inside me.

"Open," Nash commands. Without hesitation, my legs spread wide. One at a time, he grips my ankles, planting my heels along the raised ridge of the bar. "Mmm, you're so wet for me, and I'm starving."

Before I can respond, Nash latches onto my swollen flesh. Where he'd teased me at his house, he wastes no time driving my body into a swirling frenzy. My muscles convulse, and my mouth opens with my moans as I cling tight to his hair. The arch in my back curves as I buck my hips into his face, demanding everything he's willing to give.

His tongue probes inside me, bracing his forearm against my upper pelvis so his elbow and hand can keep my legs open. His assault is relentless. My body is alight with the hottest flames, writhing beneath his touch. Each new wave of pleasure draws out new mewling noises from me. My whimpers are loud with every circle of his thumb against my clit and dip of his finger inside my core to join his talented tongue. I'm seconds from tumbling over the edge, every bit of my arousal sure to coat Nash's tongue and face.

"Nash, I'm…"

He says nothing, working me harder. My lower belly tightens, my walls squeezing tighter with his probing fingers and tongue before I explode. Every nerve ending fires with my release, my grip on his hair so tight I'm surprised he doesn't cry out in pain.

"That's my girl," he whispers against my center, licking me clean before rising to his full height. His lips find mine, the taste of me on his lips becoming a new favorite these past few days. "That was one."

"One what?" I question, panting as if I just ran a marathon.

"The first time I made you come tonight," he chuckles, dampening a paper towel before cleaning me some more.

Hopping down from the counter, my knees wobble, but he holds me up. "And we're counting why?"

Sliding my shorts and underwear back up my thighs, purposely running his fingers over my flesh as he does, he leans in close once they're in place. "How many men spoke to you tonight?"

Goodness gracious, this man might kill me.

CHAPTER 34

NASH

Anxious knots twist my insides. The sweat beading at the nape of my neck and causing my shirt to stick to my back is uncomfortable. Every breath seems to come so quickly after the last, I wonder if I'll start hyperventilating soon. I haven't been this nervous since the day I took the SATs at seventeen.

I shouldn't be nervous. It's just dinner with the Hughes family. There have been hundreds over the years. Yet, for the others, I wasn't dating their daughter or sister. I wasn't fucking her day and night because minutes away from her felt like an eternity. In my mind, if I didn't take advantage of every moment now, I might lose her.

I can't lose her.

Betty pleaded with me to drive separately. An ask that nearly made me cry like a fucking chump. It told me more than I wanted to acknowledge. She still doesn't quite believe me. She still doubts that I'm in this and not going anywhere. The signs are there daily, but until today, I could pretend like we were moving past them.

Every action of mine has been with the intent of proving to her I'm in this. That we're now a *we* and will be until the day *we* die. It's impossible to say how I know she's it for me, but I do. Betty is everything to me. It's as if her confession revealed a missing piece inside me that only she could fit into.

I've talked to Hunt about it. It's like my feelings for her were a switch flipped overnight. But no one knows me like he does. He listened while I recapped twenty-three years of knowing her. *"Buddy, this is what it looks like to fall in love with a friend and the soul that matches yours. It doesn't matter that you only just figured it out. Things like this are always only a matter of time,"* he'd said. I knew my best friend could be sentimental, but this was a side of him he'd never let me see.

Parking in front of her parents' house, I release one more ragged breath before climbing out of the truck. My steps are sure as I march up to the front door, that crooked step creaking under my weight. Letting myself in the way I always have, I worry my lip, hoping I don't ruin this for Betty. Not when I am still working so hard to earn her trust.

Just act normal, Nash. Same as you've always been.

Betty isn't ready to tell everyone about us yet, and I respect that, but it doesn't mean it doesn't sting. It doesn't mean I'm not wracking my brain trying to figure out how to ensure she believes me.

"Nash!" Mr. Hughes appears around the corner, pulling me into a bear hug.

A soft laugh funnels out of me. "Hey, Mr. Hughes."

"How you holding up, son? Glad to hear your momma is doing better. You send them our best now." He points a playful finger, but I know he means business. He'll know if I don't relay the message just as he intended.

Taking a step back, I fix a few of the flowers in the bouquet I bought for Betty. Flowers of every type and color, curated just for her. The florist had thought I was insane until I explained it to her. Then she thought I was the sweetest husband alive.

I almost corrected her, but my heart and head enjoyed hearing *husband* a little too much. It wasn't something I cared about with Katherine. But attaching that innocuous word to Betty set my insides on fire. It felt right. It felt exciting.

"Beckett's out back," Mr. Hughes points a thumb over his shoulder. "He's got the grill fired up, getting ready to put the steaks on."

"Thanks, but I want to give these to Betty first." I raise the bouquet, flashing a grin that surely must have me looking like a fool.

"Ahh," Mr. Hughes snorts. "You always did know how to make my little girl smile."

Something like pride fills my chest. Maybe it shouldn't. Maybe I should be worried that he figured out there's something between us. The flowers shouldn't have given us away. I bought them last time too. "Kitchen," he cocks his head to the side, allowing me to pass without another word.

The sounds of Betty and her mother singing and laughing as they chop vegetables for a salad draw out a grin from me. Once again, images of what our life could look like together flash before my eyes.

"Hi," I interrupt, ducking into their sacred space.

Betty jumps, her hand flying to her chest. "Nash. Oh, hi," she breathes, picking up the leaves of lettuce that flew to the floor with her reaction.

I wait for her to stand before handing her the flowers. She's quick to take them from my hands, studying them with a goofy grin on her face. "Thank you," she all but whispers.

Hug me. Kiss me. Please.

Yet, she doesn't. The flowers remain clutched to her chest as if they are the most precious thing in the world. Anxious energy seems to make my body vibrate as I stand here staring at her, waiting until those brown eyes find mine. So much shines in their warm brown hue. Appreciation. Lust. Love. The same love she has always held for me is clearer now. Gratitude fills my heart that my actions and time never made it fade away.

Even when I didn't realize what it was, she's always looked at me that very same way.

"Hey, sweetheart," Mrs. Hughes pulls me out of my trance, hugging me close, then looking me over at arm's distance. "We heard about your sweet momma. She's going to be okay, sweetheart." She pats my cheek before returning to her prep. "Do you mind setting the table for me while we finish up in here?"

"Uh, no. Not at all."

Knowing my way around the kitchen, I grab the everyday plates and silverware, just as I had so many times when I was younger. It was always the kids who set the table, often rotating between me and Beckett because Betty wanted to learn how to cook.

The moment alone is necessary as emotion swells in my chest. The Hugheses and my parents have never been close friends per se, but Cole County is massive until it's not. We all know one another, and my parents knew how much time I've spent here over the years.

My mother's recent health concerns have felt like something I've had to carry alone. Sure, Hunt knew, and my parents are as positive as they can be. But my sisters haven't even bothered to come home and see her. Their phone calls stream in daily, but remain short, with just enough time to dole out the bullet points of an update before one of their children screeches in the background.

I've never cared that they wanted to have their own lives. We always wanted different things, and there's nothing wrong with that. We're all entitled to live the lives we choose, but fuck do I resent them for not caring more sometimes. Mom and Dad deserve that. They gave us everything and then some growing up. We never wanted for anything, even when times were tough. At the very least, they could show up when our mother is laid up in the hospital.

"Hey," Betty whispers, moving beside me. Her hand is light as it slides across my back, her eyes searching mine.

Dammit, I thought I'd done well enough hiding my emotions, not from her, but from the probing questions that might follow regarding my mother's prognosis. I don't want to answer those right now. We're supposed to have a nice dinner with my girlfriend's family, full of the same laughter that has always made our stomachs ache sitting around this table. That's it.

Shifting my body to face her, she's never looked more beautiful in her baby blue sundress. Taking her hand in mine, I kiss her palm, letting go just in time for Beckett to stalk through the back doors.

"Steaks are done." He raises the serving dish as if showcasing his work before setting it at the center of the table.

"I'll grab the salads," Betty spins on her heel, leaving me alone with her brother.

My palms sweat. I know she's not ready to tell her family about us, but I'm analyzing every look. Every word. Every movement. I am convinced that they know about us and are just waiting for us to confess.

It's Betty's choice. It's her family, and I don't want her saying a word until she has confidence in me, in us.

Dinner passes the way it always has, only this time I got to sneak touches along Betty's bare thigh under the table. My fingers drew tiny circles over her skin, inching higher and higher until she squirmed and shoved my hand away. My laughter timed perfectly with another of Beckett's recollections from our youth, so no one knew but us.

For a guy who barely talks outside of his house or the office, he's always the ringleader seated around his table. I wonder whether others see me in the same way.

Holding a conversation is not an issue, but standing silent in a corner is my go-to more often than not. Then you put me around the people who mean the world to me, and I can become a different person. I become the man Betty makes me want to be all the time. Loud and playful. Loving and full of life.

"Son, those steaks were done up right tonight, and that chimichurri sauce. Boom!" Mr. Hughes smacks the table.

"Okay, enough, big guy," Mrs. Hughes scolds her husband playfully.

I watch as she stands and starts rounding up the dishes before I interrupt. "Betty and I will handle that, Mama Hughes. You three head out back, and we'll join you in a few."

We need a moment alone. Rather, I need a minute alone with my woman.

"You're such a good boy," she grins before taking her husband's arm and stepping out into the warm night air.

Beckett disappears into the kitchen, carrying three beers back out with him to follow his family. It's almost a replica of the last night I'd been here, but this time, Betty isn't scuttling away from me. Her gaze lingers on my face, heat brewing in her eyes. This time we're different.

Only a few hours have passed since I last had her, but I swear I crave her as much as air. It's never enough, and my cock is hard every five minutes. It's really a problem when I'm out there trying to mend fences or wrangle spooked horses, and she's just standing there watching me in those tiny shorts and her tank tops that expose her cleavage for anyone to see.

She doesn't say a word as she rounds up our plates, and I gather the glasses. It's as if this is our everyday life, washing the dishes beside one another as she flicks water droplets at my shirt, only to giggle when I tickle her ribs.

We'd done the same after every meal at the house in Montana and these past few days at her apartment and my cabin. My woman was just as determined to spend as much time with me as I wanted to spend with her, so we avoided the Miller house. We drove separate cars and never left together.

It was awful being stuck watching her from afar and only stealing kisses in the shadows of the barn. Oddly enough, there was only one occasion we almost got caught, and it was by Ward. That was the last time Betty let me touch her in the stables.

"Scoot over, I'm getting water all over me," Betty chortles.

Her breath hitches as I grab her by the wrist and spin her around, pinning her back to the counter's edge.

"You know how much I like you wet. My words are a whispered promise against her lips before I drag her lower lip between my teeth.

A tiny sound escapes her. One that has my cock twitching in my jeans, threatening to swell if she so much as makes another peep. Her fingers sink into my hair, pulling my face down to hers, her mouth immediately opening, allowing me access to her.

The taste of her consumes me, our bodies grinding into each other when Beckett's voice booms behind us. "What the fuck are you doing?"

CHAPTER 35

NASH

My heart hammers in my chest as I spin around, shielding Betty's body with mine. My arm extends out to the side, her fingers curling around my biceps. The warmth of her breath on my back calms me as I stare her brother down, but I refuse to move.

"I asked you a question," Beckett practically growls, stalking toward us slowly, his empty beer bottle in hand.

"Beck, I can explain." I keep my tone as soft as my voice allows. Yet he still advances on us, his eyes darting from mine to a spot behind me. This is exactly what she didn't want. Even when I wasn't trying, I fucked this up.

"Betty, what the hell is going on?" Beckett ignores me, just as his sister steps from behind me, her hand blindly grabbing hold of mine.

My eyes never leave her brother. I don't think he'd do anything stupid and attack, but there's too much emotion in his eyes to predict what his next reaction will be.

A chill shoots up my arm as Betty releases my hand, slowly stepping toward her brother. "Listen to me, Beckett. Nash and I..."

"Nash and you what? Why is *my* friend basically screwing *my* little sister in our parents' kitchen?" Beckett's tone shifts. The words began as a snarl until the anger fades and they become a broken mutter. It's heartbreaking to witness. We never intended to hurt anyone, but that's what this is. Hurt. Betrayal.

He and Betty have always been close. The two of them might as well have been twins with how much time they spent together growing up and how they've always confided in one another. They still have weekly lunches that they never miss.

Betty slowly wraps her arms around her brother's middle, resting her cheek against his chest before she speaks again. She, too, keeps her tone soft. "Nash told you, it's not like that. We're... together." That pause makes my heart sink. She wasn't ready to tell them about us, and now, because I couldn't avoid kissing her, she's been forced to.

Will I ever stop hurting this woman?

"You two are dating?" Beckett's brow scrunches low, his eyes darting between me and his sister. Betty only nods, stepping out of her brother's hold. "And you weren't going to tell us?" The pain of our secret causes Beckett's words to crack. When

I didn't think I could feel any worse about the situation, I suddenly do.

"We, um, were going to tell you all tonight," Betty mumbles.

My buddy's eyes narrow on me. Surely my face is an obvious display of my surprise at her words.

Trembling fingers once again take hold of mine before she leads us out of the kitchen and onto the back patio. I want so badly to hold her. To take away the fear and anxiety that must be coursing through her right now. It wasn't supposed to be like this.

"Mom, Dad," Betty swallows hard. "Uh, we have something to tell you."

Three sets of eyes focus on my face, Beckett keeping to the doorway with his arms crossed and one ankle resting over the other. Their two dogs stand before sitting down at his feet, as if they, too, are ready for our announcement.

Inhaling deeply, my mouth opens, shuts, then stretches open again. "Mr. and Mrs. Hughes, Betty and I are dating. It's fairly new, and we weren't planning to announce it yet, but it feels right to be honest with you. Y'all have been so good to me since we met, and I want you to know how much it means to me to call Betty mine. I also want you to know I never thought about her like that until a year ago."

"And what changed then?" Mr. Hughes cocks his chin my way, his thick brows dipping low. Placing his beer bottle on the table, he leans back in his chair, crossing his arms over his chest. Beckett has never looked as much like him as he does now. Their hard expressions once again making me sweat as they wait for my answer.

I debate baring it all, explaining where we started and how I fucked up multiple times before we made it here. But I don't. Betty already wasn't prepared for this, so I'm not embarrassing her too.

My gaze meets Betty's, a hint of a smile pulling at the corners of her mouth. "Someone opened my eyes to what was right in front of me."

A tear streaks down Mrs. Hughes's cheek, a tissue dabbed there as if she'd been prepared. "Well, I, for one, am glad you both found comfort in one another. We've worried about you over the years, Nash, and our Betty has always wanted a family of her own. I think you two are well matched."

Beckett and Mr. Hughes both snap their focus on Mrs. Hughes, and every bit of tension seems to float out of our bodies.

"You're okay with us?" Betty whimpers.

"Is there a reason we shouldn't be?" Mr. Hughes interjects.

"I—" Betty begins, squeezing my hand. Releasing her, I pull her into my side, kissing the top of her head before lowering into the seat behind me. She sinks into my lap without a fight, her arms wrapping tightly around my middle.

"No. There's not, but I'm also not naïve enough to think there might not be some hesitation because of my age or..." My words drift into the space between us. Maybe I've said too much.

Mrs. Hughes waves her crumpled tissue through the air. "Oh, nonsense. This man here has almost fifteen years on me. We care how you treat our daughter, not that you have a head start on gray hairs."

I nearly choke on my laughter. Betty's eyes flash wide at her mother's comment. Beckett doubles over, coughing loudly to hide his own laughter, and just like that, all is right in the world.

"Thank you," she whispers in my ear, kissing my cheek.

Brushing my lips against her temple, I hold her a little closer. "I told you I'd prove how much I want you, Andromeda."

"Okay, enough of that canoodlin'," Mr. Hughes huffs. "Nash, you ran scared last dinner, and I didn't get to beat you in trivia. You're not escaping this time."

We all groan, knowing this is going to be a long night. It's the game we've always played. Facts bound us together over the years. Mr. Hughes acts as if I've ever beaten him in trivia. I haven't, not once. They're a family of brainiacs.

But there's one fact I know without a shadow of a doubt. I am in love with his daughter, and there's nothing I wouldn't do for her.

Our night stretches well past midnight. Betty's yawns signaling me to call the game. "You win, Mr. Hughes. I need to get this one home."

"You be safe now," Mrs. Hughes pulls me into her, squeezing me harder than she ever has before. I hold her back, wishing for a lifetime of this. These feelings never lived inside me with Katherine and her family. We liked each other just fine, but they never felt like home.

Beckett pulls me into his hold next, clapping my back harder than necessary. "You hurt my sister, and I'll make sure one of your bulls pierces a lung."

"Love you too, Beck," I clap his back. Both of us grin like the fools we've always been together. He'd been the one I worried about most. We were friends first, and he's always been protective of his sister. I wouldn't have left her because he disapproved, but I'd have been heartbroken to lose his friendship just the same. Beckett has always been my brother, and maybe now, someday soon, we'll make it true. "For what it's worth, I'm glad it's you, too," he whispers before gathering up the game pieces and returning them to the box.

Turning, I catch the tail end of Mr. Hughes's words to his daughter. The two embracing as if they may never see one another again. "...found a good one. Don't get in your own way. You're allowed to be happy again."

My girl sniffles, pulling away from her dad before looping her arm around my back. Then we're off.

We are different now, as if we're finally this real entity that has a chance to grow.

Soon we will. Soon she'll be mine in every way, and it won't just be us.

CHAPTER 36

BETTY

It's been six weeks since Nash and I told everyone about us.

Most days, I can tell myself he's really in it this time. That we're going to make it, and all my dreams are coming true. He's given me no reason to believe otherwise. Only I haven't seen him since the last rodeo. His business took him back to Montana and then to a few other states.

I miss him so much it hurts. In just a few short weeks, I'd grown used to sleeping beside him every night, regardless of whose bed it was in. Then one night, he just wasn't beside me anymore. We speak every day and video chat, but it's not the same.

My skin misses the feel of his and the warmth of his lips on mine. The only thing getting me through is knowing he'll be back this week.

It's the second-to-last rodeo of the season, so there are some massive cash prizes on the table, and last chances to qualify for the big leagues. It's the best of the best who will be here competing, including Gray, but it's a busy time, too. The professional promotions have their own finals right around the corner, with competitions taking place every weekend.

He's exhausted, and I feel horrible for not being there with him. He asked; I declined. But I had responsibilities here—the inn, the bar, my loyalty to Cole County.

"Hey, sweetheart," my dad's voice pulls me out of my wandering thoughts, each one centered on the man I love more and more each day.

We hug briefly before he rests his elbows on the fence, staring off into the distance beside me. A lazy grin pulls at the corners of his mouth, but he says nothing.

"Dad, what are you doing here?"

My dad rarely comes out to Boulder Ranch these days. He was never a rodeo guy and hates crowds. "Can't I want to see my only daughter?"

I give him a wry grin. He's up to something. It's possible that my mom put him up to giving me the motivational speech he's about to deliver, but no one gives them better than he does. If the sports season was going awry, it was Papa Hughes who was called in to bring back the team spirit.

"Of course you can." Nudging his shoulder, we stand in silence for a long beat as the sun sets behind the trees.

The soft blue fades into shades of eggplant as the crest of orange narrows with each passing second. I've always loved sunsets. It was the gateway to my favorite time of the day. Only in the dark could I marvel at the universe beyond the earth we live on. It felt like the only way I could experience magic until Nash became mine.

Damn, I miss him.

"It's beautiful out here," my father sighs. The words drift out into the field where we watch the horses graze freely. The moment is peaceful, serene.

"It is. There's no place like it in the world." The words pass my lips, but in truth, I don't know that for a fact. I'm thirty-three and I haven't been anywhere.

"You shouldn't say that until you actually see the world, sweetheart." My head whips in his direction. "Yah know, that just makes sense," he clears his throat.

My heart races, unsure if I'm hearing what my father is trying to say correctly. "My life is here," I whisper.

My father finally pushes off the fence, turning to face me. "A piece of your life is here. It'll always be here, Betty. But there's a whole world out there waiting for you to explore and a man who would gladly carry you around it on his back if he had to."

That guilt I'd pushed down a long time ago rises. The Hugheses don't leave Cole County. I've bound myself to that history even when no one told me to. Even when my heart begged and pleaded for more, I denied it. I followed our roots.

Nash once asked me why I insisted I was like Andromeda. Back then, I never had the heart to explain to anyone why I felt like a chained woman. It's always been a part of my family history, my last name, and my inability to stand up for what I wanted and who I wanted to be. I've allowed myself glimpses into a world outside that cage, but never shoved my hands through the small crack and torn it wide open.

My head drops, not wanting to have this conversation. "You know why." The words come out in a defeated huff, and I hate that once again I'm not standing up for myself. That I feel like I can't.

"Beatrice, you don't have to be us or anyone else. You get to be you. Sweetheart, you earned an astronomy degree, and you have been fascinated by the stars your entire life. You think we didn't know you were itching to get out of here. Your mother and I have been waiting for you to take the leap. We've been hoping you'd find the bravery."

Watery eyes meet my father's. I never needed permission to break free. It was always my choice to go, but I also wanted everyone else to be happy. I wanted to uphold the family name.

The first tear slips free as I wrap my arms around my father's neck, hugging him tight. "Thanks, Daddy. I just wanted to make everyone proud," I sniffle.

"Make yourself proud, Betty Major." I pull back, meeting his stare once more. "We should have never nicknamed you minor. You are going to do amazing things and live the major life you deserve."

The floodgates break open, tears streaming down my face as I rest my head on my father's shoulder once again.

Once again, my world shifts for the better.

Things are changing, and it feels so good.

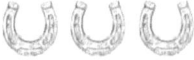

A soft crash in the Miller house living room causes me to bolt upright in bed. The house and the cabins are empty. No one should arrive until tomorrow.

Please don't be another burst pipe or the ceiling collapsing.

Glancing at my phone, it's just after one in the morning. I'm too tired for this.

Another bang reverberates through the house, punctuated by a man's grunt. Who the hell is here?

I doubt any of the ranch hands are still here, and no way the Garrisons would come in here at this time of night. They both have pregnant wives at home.

Swinging my legs over the edge of the bed, I listen for additional sounds, my heart hammering so loud my ears are ringing. Maybe an animal got in, and it wasn't a man I heard. Maybe it's just the sounds of this old house.

Slowly twisting my bedroom doorknob, I edge the door open, peering around the frame into the empty hallway. The house is dark and quiet. There doesn't seem to be anyone here but me.

Every horror movie warning comes flooding in. Don't explore. Don't call out. But I'll be damned if someone breaks in here.

Tip-toeing into the hallway, a sound like ruffled clothing drifts from the living room. Balling my hands into fists, I creep toward it, doing my best to keep my breathing quiet. I know how to defend myself. Whoever it is won't get away without a fight.

The moment I turn the corner, the light flashes on, revealing Nash leaning against the doorframe, rubbing his shin.

"Dammit, Nash, you almost gave me a heart attack."

He says nothing, reaching for me, his mouth on mine before gripping behind my thighs. My legs wrap around his waist, holding his head in place as I kiss him like I need to breathe.

His palms cup my ass, hoisting me higher while he marches toward the bedroom. "Andromeda, I missed you so much," he mumbles against my lips.

"Me too. I hated being away from you." I hadn't planned on admitting that to him when I saw him again, but the words broke free. Maybe it's a side effect of the talk my dad and I had earlier.

He peppers open-mouthed kisses along my jaw before capturing my mouth again. We both can barely breathe as he pulls away. "I wish you'd come with me." He speaks the words against my throat, flicking his tongue up the column before sucking my flesh between his lips.

Our bodies fall to the bed, his frame nestled between my legs. My hips grind up into him, seeking the friction of his rock-hard length. I want his skin on mine. I need him inside me, claiming me as his, making me chant his name like the only prayer I've ever needed.

Running my tongue across his bottom lip, I bring his mouth to mine once more, only pulling away when I'm in desperate need of air. "Next time I will."

The world seems to stop, Nash rising, so his weight no longer crushes me. "What?"

Running my palm over his short beard, my eyes lock with his. "Next time, I will come with you. These past weeks without you were awful. I never thought I could miss someone so much. So if you ask me to come next time, I will."

There's no identifying the emotions that flash in Nash's blue eyes as he tucks my hair behind my ear and slowly bends to kiss me softly.

"You have no idea what you've given me," he breathes.

"Tell me."

His lips brush mine again before he whispers, "Everything."

My love for him swirls inside me. It's not the same crush I'd held onto for decades. It's not the infatuation and the day-dreams. Being with Nash for real has allowed genuine feelings to grow. The type that never go away and nothing or no one can ever erase. "Make love to me," I whisper.

For once, Nash takes his time removing our clothes and sinking inside me. Our pace is slow. Our connection is like nothing I've ever felt with anyone. I never want this moment to end. I never want to lose him.

We come together, his name on my lips and mine on his. Only when he's cleaned us, pulling me into his chest, does he speak again. "I'm mad at you, Andromeda."

A jaw-cracking yawn stretches my mouth wide. "Why?"

"I wanted to say, I love you first." He kisses my knuckles, pulling the blankets up over us.

"But I—" Pushing up to my elbow, I'm ready to argue that my confession from a year ago doesn't count as I glare down at him. But I stop when he flashes his teeth in an eye-crinkling smile. "It's about time."

CHAPTER 37

NASH

The last thing a distributor ever wants is for something to go wrong on rodeo night. This weekend has been an absolute catastrophe. In all the years I've assisted Pop, something like this has never happened. Never have I felt so weighed down by circumstances I couldn't have controlled, yet will reflect on me regardless.

Anything that could go wrong, did.

At the gym this morning, some asshole didn't secure his weights, and the thing went flying into my arm. River put me in a sling.

We found one of the horses lethargic in the stables, and the vet is still examining him.

Two of our bulls, which were shoe-ins for the professional tournaments, underperformed. Given my current luck, I'll likely receive a call saying they're no longer wanted.

My fucking arm is throbbing. The handful of Tylenol I popped is doing nothing to ease the pain. And the tension coiling my shoulders tight is only making it worse.

I'm worn out and on the edge of losing my shit as I wander back to the barn. Fortunately, the night is over, and I can just go the fuck home and sleep it off. But damn, this was not how I wanted to close out the season when everything in my life seems to be aligning.

"Rough night out there," a voice calls from across the barn. My head pops up in search of the source.

"That's putting it nicely," I grunt in Reed's direction. The guy is one of the best damn bull-fighters I've ever met. He's quick on his feet and can anticipate not only the bull's moves but also the riders and his counterparts.

For a guy who comes from wealthy northern roots and never stepped foot on a ranch before he came here, he's a natural. We've grabbed a beer a few times with Gray and some of the other ranch hands, so I know all about him. If he keeps himself fit and young, he'll have a nice, long career here.

But tonight, I'm hoping he doesn't ask me to join them at the Thirsty Pony. I need my bed and my woman. That's it.

He comes to a stop in front of me. His blue eyes are a colder version of mine with their faded hue. They remind me of ice and unforgiveness, yet he's one of the nicest guys I've ever met. "If it's any consolation," he drops a palm to my good shoulder.

"I heard a few bigwigs out there want to meet you. They were impressed with your professionalism."

Usually, I'll hang back for a few minutes, shake hands, and mingle as necessary. But not tonight. The performances and my pain had me too much on edge. The vet diagnosed our horse with an infection, so he will probably miss the rest of the season. There's nothing left in me to give these people tonight.

"Nash! You in here? Nash!" Betty's voice settles my soul as she comes waltzing around the corner.

"I'll see you later," Reed waves behind him.

"Bye," Betty calls after him. "Hey, how's the pain?" She runs her palm over my free arm, her eyes soft as they search mine. Why does her touch have this dual effect on me? She riles me up and calms me down. With her around, none of the bad shit matters. It's just her and me.

"Hurts like hell, but I'm better now that you're here." She only rolls her eyes, swatting my chest as I curl away from her, chuckling. "Really, though." I kiss her knuckles the way I often do. "I'm always better with you around."

Her grin spreads so wide her eyes become slits in the overhead barn lights. "Me too. But I'm here on strict orders from your father."

"My father?" I cock a brow.

"Mmhmm. I'm taking you home. He'll be here in a few to wrap everything up."

She'd done this. My woman knew I was hurt and that the night had been horrible, and she just wanted to take care of me. I'd called Pop various times tonight, keeping him apprised of how things were going, but I hadn't mentioned my injury. It didn't seem important. There was a job to do, and I was going to get it done. It's what I've always done.

Work came first, and I came last.

Tonight, Betty is putting me first. So, I let her take my hand and lead me out of the barn. "Um, the house is that way," I groan against the movement jostling my arm.

"I'm aware. We're going to the cabin."

"What happened to 'We have guests, I can't leave?'" I let my voice pitch high, playfully imitating hers. She only snorts, leading me to my truck and digging my keys out of my front pocket. "Baby, stop feeling me up out here. I'll be so embarrassed if I drop you trying to lift you with one good arm."

She leans into my chest, her fingertips steepled against my pecs as my keys jingle. "Nash, you'll know when I'm taking advantage of you."

Fuck, my cock twitches just imagining Betty having her way with me. I'd expected her to be timid in the bedroom, but she's the opposite. She submits to me as much as she tells me exactly how she wants it. The give and take serves as a perfect balance for us. It's evened out my rough tendencies and allowed me to worship her as I should.

I never wanted to be a passionate lover with Katherine or anyone else. I wanted to fuck while still leaving my partner sated. But that's where it ended. It wasn't about their needs; it was about mine. It was only important for me to leave them satisfied, because that meant I had done my job.

It's always about getting the job done.

Our drive back to the cabin is the reset I need, genuine happiness swelling in my chest. Tonight had been shit, but Betty made me see the silver lining in it all. Three of our animals may not have performed tonight, but at least it's the end of the season. They've had convincing performances otherwise, and that will count for more. One off night won't ruin it all.

I've already received several emails in my inbox with other promotions and rodeos from all over the country, all of whom want to discuss business with us. I'm the new blood distribution needs.

I'd always thought my perspective on life, and how I was living it, was solid. There were no changes to make because it was working. Betty opened my eyes. There's more than obligation and work. Approaching life so robotically you're not living isn't what I want anymore.

We pull up the drive, the two lights bordering the front door of the cabin casting a soft glow over the three steps leading to the entrance. "Baby, you have to carry me inside," I pout, as she reaches for her door.

"Nash Donovan, you're a big baby. Get out of this damn truck. You stink and need a shower."

A barking laugh bursts out of me as I exit the truck and rush up the stairs ahead of her. Digging in the pocket she'd thankfully ignored, I pull out a key decorated in purples and blues, dotted with stars. It's attached to a globe that lights up when you hit the button.

Handing it to her, she stares down at it. "What is this?" Her voice is small as she turns the globe over in her fingers, her thumb tracing the tiny lines of the countries.

"It's your key to this cabin. The globe is because you've always wanted to see if the stars look different in other places. If you let me, I'll take you anywhere so you can find out."

Tears well in her eyes as she looks up at me, her bottom lip wobbling. "Nash..."

"You don't need to say anything. Beatrice," I stroke my thumb over her cheek, catching her tears. "You gave me life, and all I want is to give you your dreams. So, please let me."

She turns away from me, sliding the key into the lock before stepping inside. I follow on her heels, locking the door behind us. "So does this mean you're expecting me to cancel my lease?" I'm surprised as she spins back to face me, her arms looping around my neck as she pushes up onto her toes.

"Only if you love me."

Our lips brush in the softest kiss that speaks of forever. "Do you know what I want?" she grins.

"Tell me."

Her grin draws wider, those brown eyes sparkling. "To wake up next to you every day, under every sky."

"And do you know what I want?" I ask, running my palm along her side. She shakes her head animatedly, never breaking her stare. "I just want you."

EPILOGUE

BETTY

2 *months later...*

Packing is absolutely the worst activity known to man. Where had all these clothes and the shoes even come from?

Nash and I have three large suitcases laid open on the bed and a fourth, medium-sized one, open on the floor.

Piles of clothes sit everywhere. What do you pack for a five-week trip to Europe? It was a surprise from Nash shortly after I moved into the cabin. He's yet to confirm whether it was something he'd been planning or if it was a spur-of-the-moment decision.

It didn't matter to me. This will be my first time outside the United States. I'm finally going to get to see the stars. Prague, Great Britain, Spain, Scotland, Greece, and the Netherlands. It's just the first trip of many we've talked about. I'd never known Nash wanted to travel the world, too, so it was a pleasant surprise.

The buzz of Nash's phone on the dresser pulls me out of my overstimulated panic. "Nash, your phone!" I shout. He's somewhere in this cabin. It's pretty small, so I honestly can't say what's taking him so long.

"Can you answer it for me?" he calls back.

Clicking the green button, I place the phone to my ear. "Hello. Nash Donovan's phone."

"Oh, is this Betty? So nice to finally speak with you," a gruff male voice comes through the line.

"Thank you. May I ask who's calling?" Balancing the phone between my shoulder and ear, I toss my tennis shoes into the suitcase on the floor.

The slam of a car door sounds through the phone before the man answers. "Oh, yes. I'm Mr. Donovan's realtor. I was calling to let him know an offer came in on the house, well over asking." There's an upbeat tone to his delivery, as if there's cause for celebration.

My mouth twists to the side, attempting to process what he just said. "Um, what house?" Had Nash sold the cabin and not told me? Where will we live? I hadn't even known it was on the market. There's a shuffle of papers in the background before he reads off the address for Nash's Montana home. "Oh," I gasp. "Um, thank you. I'll let him know."

Ending the call, I'm in a trance as I place the phone back on the dresser, staring off into space.

We never talked about him selling the Montana house. For the past few months, I've traveled everywhere with Nash, and we've stayed there most of the time, always in the bedroom beside his. I've never told him how much that meant to me. He'd carved out a space that was just ours, though he'd shared the house with his ex-wife.

"Who was that?" He slides into the room with an armful of towels fresh out of the dryer. The ocean scent of our dryer sheets fills the air, and I inhale deeply, allowing a lazy grin to pull at the corners of my mouth before I remember the call I just answered.

"Your realtor. He said the house sold well over asking." Nash's jaw works as he looks down at me. The hurt must be evident on my face. "You never told me you were selling the house."

Dropping the towels on the bed, he pulls me into his arms, a single finger placed beneath my chin, forcing my gaze up to meet his. "I didn't think it mattered. I don't need that house anymore."

"But why?"

Soft lips brush mine, peppering kisses at the corners of my mouth before he speaks again. "Because, Beatrice Hughes, you're my home, and if I'm lucky enough, you'll be my wife. That house doesn't matter because wherever you are is where I'll be."

My whole damn heart just melts as I sink into him, fisting the back of his shirt in my hands. We say nothing as he holds me, our bodies rocking side to side until I'm sure I won't cry again. I swear this man has made me shed more tears out of heartbreak, sadness, frustration, and now love than one would think possible.

"Will you buy something else out there?" I ask, pulling away once again, folding clothes I'm not even sure I want to pack.

He only shrugs. "Maybe."

"Nash, come on. Your business is out there. There has to be a plan." My fingers grip the suitcase, staring into those pools of blue I've always gotten lost in.

"I can do business from anywhere." Glancing over at the clock, an electrical jolt seems to run through him. His spine suddenly straightens, his jaw flexing hard.

"What's wrong?" I pant, unsure why he looks like there's a fire under his ass as he disappears into the closet, reappearing with a suit. "Are you taking that with you?" I wrinkle my nose.

"Nope, I'm putting it on. There's a dress in there for you, too. Hurry up," he swats my ass. "Our ride will be here in ten minutes."

I swear, this morning is giving me whiplash as I slink into the closet, pulling a white garment bag from the rack and tugging the zipper down. This hadn't been here this morning when I was yanking clothes out of the closet. Had it?

A simple lace fitted dress with pearl beading and subtle shimmer stares back at me. "Nash, what is this?" I reappear from the closet, holding the dress as far away from me as possible. My eyes scan the room, realizing Nash isn't standing there anymore. "Nash?"

"Down here, Andromeda."

My gaze tracks down, and right there at my feet, Nash is down on one knee with a goofy grin on his face. "Nash..."

"I feel like I've spilled a lot of my guts, so I don't have any good words left right now. But you know the important things. I was an idiot not to fall for you from day one, but I'm glad I finally did. You gave me chance after chance, and I didn't deserve them. So, Andromeda, how about you switch those chains to me? Marry me, Betty."

My world seems to stop. Every dream, fantasy, and scene that played out in my mind always led us here. After so long, I never believed it would happen, and then Nash wanted me. Still, I kept that hope tucked away. I wasn't strong enough to cling to it out of fear. "I was wrong too," I whisper, but I hold out my hand to him. The violet-colored diamond shimmers inside its black box before he slips it free.

"Is that a yes?" he asks, the ring hovering a hair's breadth from the tip of my finger.

"In every universe, yes," I sob, before tackling him to the floor. His lips meet mine, and the two of us laugh in a heap.

Staring at the ring, I'm wondering how we got here. How did my drunken confession get me to the man of my dreams? "Nash, one question," I grunt as we climb up from the floor.

"Anything."

"Why now?"

Those blue eyes find mine. "You didn't think I was going to stare up at the stars around the world and not have the brightest one as my wife, did you?"

THANK YOU FOR READING!
YOUR NEXT READ IS JUST A PAGE AWAY...

ALSO BY BRITTON BRINKLEY

Misfits Trilogy (with L.A. Scott)

Misunderstood

Misfortune

Accepted

Night Life Duology

Night Life

Night Life 2: Will to Fight

The Company Series

The Tournament

The Target (COMING 1-19-26)

Disavowed Birthright Trilogy

Rise of the Grisym

Dimmer of the Light

Master of the Dark (COMING 2026)

Fall of the Phoenix Trilogy

Feathers of Truth

Feathers of Destruction

Feathers of Change (COMING 12-19-25)

Scarlet Hearts

Scarlet Hearts

Broken Promises (COMING 2026)

Boulder Ranch

Ride Me

Buck Me (by Ashley Willow)

Want Me

Love Me (by Ashley Willow)

Save Me (COMING 4-20-26)

Hunt Me (by Ashley Willow – COMING 4-20-26)

Dagger & Sword

The Shadows That Shackle (COMING 2025)

Baudelaire Blood
Venetia (COMING 2025)

The Loyals
The Loyals (COMING 2025)

Crux Duology
Don't Scream (COMING 2025)

About the Author

Britton Brinkley was born in New Jersey and now lives in Northern Virginia.

Growing up an avid reader, the sciences and ancient civilizations mesmerized her. She has always loved immersing herself in new worlds. Britton now enjoys creating her own with her writing buddies Jay Gatsby and the little psycho Artemis Prime (the cats).

When she isn't writing, she's likely either reading, watching Criminal Minds, or some other true crime show on Investigation Discovery.

Learn More at BrittonBrinkley.com